The Lagoon

Ruskin Bond has been writing for over sixty years, and now has over 120 titles in print—novels, collections of short stories, poetry, essays, anthologies and books for children. His first novel, *The Room on the Roof*, received the prestigious John Llewellyn Rhys Prize in 1957. He has also received the Padma Shri (1999), the Padma Bhushan (2014) and two awards from Sahitya Akademi—one for his short stories and another for his writings for children. In 2012, the Delhi government gave him its Lifetime Achievement Award.

Born in 1934, Ruskin Bond grew up in Jamnagar, Shimla, New Delhi and Dehradun. Apart from three years in the UK, he has spent all his life in India, and now lives in Mussoorie with his adopted family.

The Lagoon

Selected and Compiled by
RUSKIN BOND

First published by
Rupa Publications India Pvt. Ltd 2017
161-B/4, Gulmohar House,
Yusuf Sarai Community Centre,
New Delhi 110049

Sales centres:
Bengaluru Chennai
Hyderabad Kolkata Mumbai

Copyright © Ruskin Bond 2017

This is a work of fiction. Names, characters, places and incidents are either the product of the author's imagination or are used fictitiously, and any resemblance to any actual persons, living or dead, events or locales is entirely coincidental.

All rights reserved.
No part of this publication may be reproduced, transmitted, or stored in a retrieval system, in any form or by any means, electronic, mechanical, photocopying, recording or otherwise, without the prior permission of the publisher.

P-ISBN: 978-81-291-4527-7
E-ISBN: 000-00-000-0023-7

Seventh impression 2026

10 9 8 7

The moral right of the author has been asserted.

Printed in India

This book is sold subject to the condition that it shall not, by way of trade or otherwise, be lent, resold, hired out, or otherwise circulated, without the publisher's prior consent, in any form of binding or cover other than that in which it is published.

CONTENTS

Introduction	*vii*
Happiness *Guy de Maupassant*	1
The Philosopher in the Apple Orchard *Anthony Hope*	9
The Lady with the Dog *Anton Chekhov*	20
Maru *Henry de Vere Stacpoole*	42
Mary Ansell *Martin Armstrong*	60
The Last Leaf *O. Henry*	72
The Duenna *Marie Belloc Lowndes*	80
The Pillar of Heliodoros *Anonymous*	97
The Girl on the Train *Ruskin Bond*	113

The Lagoon   117
Joseph Conrad
The Box Tunnel   135
Charles Reade

INTRODUCTION

What is it about love stories that make them eternal favourites with readers? In plays and poetry, short stories and novels, love is perhaps one of the most popular themes. Sometimes happy, oftentimes tragic, stories of love and romance bring out almost every facet of human behaviour. Think of the classic love stories and you will find joy, grief, jealousy, betrayal, ecstasy, all coming together to make them immortal works of literature.

It is not just the emotions, love stories also work across the barriers of age and time. Who among us has not heard or read the story of Helen of Troy and Paris, or Nala and Damayanti, or Romeo and Juliet. From books to the screen, these stories have played a large part in much of our understanding of romantic love. Of course, when it comes to real life, we may find that love can also be in the prosaic—when you make sure she is warm and comforted in a fever, or when you cannot wait to rush home to celebrate a good day at work with him. But then the minute details of everyday life was never the stuff of epics.

In this collection, I have included stories that delve into the darker shades of love as well as the lighter, happier side. The story by Maupassant, 'Happiness', for one, though by a writer who has written plenty of not so cheerful stories, is one of love that lasts into old age. 'Maru' by H. De Vere

Stacpoole takes place in the Pacific Islands and is sweet yet tinged with sadness. I also wanted the collection to have a dash of the epic romances, so there is the story of Nala and Damayanti that was nearly doomed but had a happy ending. Also included is 'The Pillar of Heliodoros', an unusual tale set in a period of Indian history.

There are also the sad yet evergreen stories from writers such as Thomas Hardy, Joseph Conrad and O. Henry. 'The Lagoon' with its white man in the dark unknown setting of a Malayan jungle, hearing a story of love and death is classic Conrad. O. Henry's 'Last Leaf' has been a favourite with many people. I also particularly enjoyed Anthony Hope's 'The Philosopher in the Apple Orchard' where the bookish philosopher knows not just how he manages to ruin his chances at love forever.

It would have been nice if some works by great women writers like Austen and the Brontes could have been included here. Alas, they mostly wrote in the larger canvas of a novel and not short stories. I have seen many women readers go misty-eyed at the mention of Heathcliff and Fitzwilliam Darcy. I remember my own first reading of *Wuthering Heights* at quite a young age, and how I read it through the night, unable to set aside the tortured love story of Heathcliff and Cathy for something as mundane as sleep.

With this collection of stories, I hope readers will find the particular shade of love that they enjoy the most, too. After all, falling in love, again and again, is what keeps us alive and human.

Ruskin Bond

HAPPINESS

Guy de Maupassant

It was teatime before the lights were brought in. The sky was all rosy with sunset and shimmering with gold dust. The villa looked down upon the Mediterranean, which lay without ripple or quiver, like a vast sheet of burnished metal, smooth and shining in the fading daylight. The irregular outline of the distant mountains on the right stood out black against the pale purple background of the western sky.

The conversation turned on love, that old familiar topic, and remarks that had been made many times before, were being offered once again. The gentle melancholy of the twilight diffused a languorous charm and created an atmosphere to tender emotion. The word 'love,' constantly reiterated, now in a man's virile voice, now in a woman's delicate tones, seemed to dominate the little drawing-room, hovering like a bird, brooding like a spirit.

'Is it possible to remain faithful to one love year after year?'

Some said yes, some said no. Distinctions were made, limits defined, and instances cited. The minds of all, men and women alike, were surging with a host of disturbing memories, which trembled on their lips, but which they dared not utter. Their emotion expressed itself in the deep and ardent interest with which they discussed this commonplace, yet sovereign, passion, this tender and mysterious bond between two beings.

Suddenly someone, with his eyes on the distant prospect, exclaimed:

'Oh, look over there. What can it be?'

On the skyline, a great blurred mass of grey was rising out of the sea. The ladies sprang to their feet and gazed in surprise at this startling thing that they had never seen before.

'It is Corsica,' someone explained. 'It is visible two or three times a year in certain exceptional atmospheric conditions. When the air is perfectly clear the mists of water vapour, which usually veil the horizon, are lifted.'

The ridges of the mountains could be faintly discerned, and some thought that they could make out even the snow on the peaks.

This sudden apparition of a phantom world, emerging from the sea, produced on those who witnessed it a disquieting impression, a feeling of uneasiness, almost of consternation.

An old gentleman, hitherto silent, exclaimed:

'That very island which has risen from the waters as if in response to our conversation, reminds me of a curious experience. It was there that I came upon a wonderful instance of faithful love, a love that was incredibly happy. This is the story:

'Five years ago I paid a visit to Corsica. Although visible now and then, like today, from the coast of France, less is known of that wild island than of America, and it seems almost more remote. Picture to yourselves a world still in a state of chaos, a raging sea of mountains, intersected by narrow gorges with rushing torrents. Instead of plains, there are vast, rolling sweeps of granite and gigantic undulations of the earth, overgrown with bush and great forests of chestnut trees and pines. It is a virgin country, desolate, uncultivated, in spite of an occasional village planted like a heap of rocks on a mountain top. There is no agriculture, industry, or art. You never come upon a scrap of wood-carving or sculpture, or any relic, showing in the Corsicans of old a taste, whether primitive or cultured, for graceful and beautiful things. It is this that strikes you most forcibly in that superb but austere country, its hereditary indifference to that striving after exquisite forms, which we call Art. In Italy, every palace is not only full of masterpieces, but is itself a masterpiece; in Italy, marble, wood, bronze, iron, metals, stone, all testify to the genius of man, and even the humblest relics of antiquity, that lie about in old houses, reveal this divine passion for beauty. Italy is to all of us a beloved and sacred land, because it displays convincingly the energy, grandeur, power and triumph of creative intelligence.

'And opposite her shores lies wild Corsica, just as she was in her earliest days. There a man leads his own life in his rude cottage, indifferent to everything that does not directly concern himself or his family quarrels. And he still retains the defects and qualities of primitive races. Passionate, vindictive, frankly bloodthirsty, he is at the same time hospitable, generous, faithful, ingenuous. He opens his door to the stranger and repays the most trifling act of kindness with loyal friendship.

'For a whole month I had been wandering all over this magnificent island, and I had a feeling of having reached the end of the world. There are no inns, no taverns, no roads.

Mule tracks lead up to hamlets that cling to the mountainsides and look down upon windings canons, from whose depths rises in an evening the deep, muffled roar of torrents. The wanderer knocks at the door of a house and asks for a night's hospitality. He takes his place at his host's frugal board, sleeps beneath his humble roof, and the next day the master of the house escorts his guest to the outskirts of the village, where they shake hands and part.

'One evening, after a ten hours' tramp, I reached a little solitary dwelling at the upper end of a valley, which, a mile lower, fell away abruptly to the sea. It was a ravine of intense dreariness, walled in by bleak mountains, rising steeply on either side, and covered with bush, fallen rocks and lofty trees. Near the hut there were some vines and a small garden, and at a little distance, some tall chestnut trees. It was enough to support life, and indeed amounted to a fortune on that poverty-stricken island.

'I was met by an old woman of severe aspect and unusual cleanliness. Her husband rose from a straw-bottomed chair, bowed to me, and then resumed his seat without a word.

'"Pray excuse him," said his wife. "He is deaf. He is eighty-two."

'To my surprise, she spoke French like a Frenchwoman. "You are not a native of Corsica?" I asked.

'"No, we are from the mainland, but we have lived here for fifty years."

'A wave of horror and dismay swept over me at the thought of those fifty years spent in that gloomy cranny, so far from towns and places where men live. An old shepherd entered, and we all sat down to supper, which consisted of a single course, thick broth containing potatoes, bacon and cabbages all cooked together. When the short meal was over I took a seat before the door. I was weighed down by the melancholy aspect of that forbidding landscape and by that feeling of depression which at times overtakes the traveller on a dismal evening in dreary surroundings, a foreboding that the end of everything, the end of existence, the end of the world, is at hand. Suddenly the appalling wretchedness of life is borne in upon us; the isolation of each one of us; the hollowness of everything; the black loneliness of the heart, which is lulled and deceived by its own imaginings to the brink of the grave.

'Presently the old woman rejoined me, and with the curiosity which lingers even in the serenest soul, she began to question me.

'"So you come from France?"

'"Yes, I am on a pleasure trip."

'"I suppose you live in Paris."

'"No, my home is Nancy."

'At this she seemed to be seized by some violent emotion, and yet I cannot explain how it was that I saw, or rather felt, her agitation.

'"Your home is Nancy?" she repeated slowly.

'Her husband appeared in the doorway, with the impassive air that deaf people have.

'"Never mind about him," she continued, "he cannot hear us."

'After a pause she resumed:

'"Then you know people at Nancy?"

'"Yes, nearly everyone."

'"Do you know the Sainte-Allaizes?"

'"Very well indeed. They were friends of my father's."

"'What is your name?'

'I told her. She looked at me searchingly. Then, in the low voice of one conjuring up the past:

"'Yes, yes, I remember perfectly. And what has become of the Brisemares?"

"'They are all dead."

"'Ah! And did you know the Sirmonts?"

"'Yes, the last of them is a General now."

'She was quivering with excitement, with pain, with mingled emotions, strong, sacred, impossible to describe, with a strange yearning to break the silence, to utter all the secrets hitherto locked away in her heart, to speak about those people, whose very names shook her to the soul.

"'Henri de Sirmont. Yes, I know," she exclaimed. "He is my brother."

'I glanced at her in amazement. Suddenly I remembered.

'Long ago there had been a terrible scandal among the Lorraine aristocracy. Suzanne de Sirmont, a beautiful and wealthy girl, had eloped with a non-commissioned officer in the Hussar regiment commanded by her father. The son of a peasant, but for all that a fine figure in his blue pelisse, this common soldier had captivated his Colonel's daughter. No doubt, she had had opportunities of seeing him, admiring him, and falling in love with him, as she watched the squadrons trooping past. But how had she contrived to speak to him? How had they managed to meet and come to an understanding? How had she ventured to convey to him that she loved him? No one ever knew.

'No suspicion had been aroused. At the end of the soldier's term of service they disappeared together one night. A search was made for them; but without result. Nothing was ever heard of them again and the family looked upon her as dead.

'And now I had found her in this desolate valley.

'"I remember perfectly," I said at last. "You are Mademoiselle Suzanne."

'She nodded. Tears welled from her eyes. Then, with a glance towards the old man, who was standing motionless on the threshold of his hut:

'"And that is my husband."

'"Then I realized that she still loved him, that she still beheld him with eyes that had not lost their illusion.

'"I trust that you have been happy?" I ventured.

'In a voice straight from the heart she answered:

'"Yes, very happy. He has made me very happy. I have never regretted anything."

'I gazed at her in sympathetic surprise, marvelling at the power of love. This well-bred, wealthy girl had followed that humble peasant, and had stooped to his level. She had submitted to an existence destitute of all the graces, luxuries, and refinements of life. She had conformed to his simple ways. And she still loved him. She had become a peasant woman, in bonnet and cotton gown. She sat on a straw-bottomed chair at a wooden table, and supped on a broth of cabbages, potatoes and bacon, served in an earthenware dish. At night she lay on a palliasse by his side. She had never had a thought for anything but her lover. And she regretted nothing, neither jewels, silks and satins, luxuries, cushioned chairs, the warmth and perfume of tapestried rooms, nor downy couches so grateful to weary limbs. He was her one desire. As long as he was there she asked no more of life.

'A mere girl, she had sacrificed her whole future, the world, and those who had brought her up and loved her. All alone with him, she had come to this wild ravine. And he had been all in all to her. He had satisfied her heart's desires, its dreams, its endless longings, its undying hopes. He had filled her whole life with bliss from beginning to end. She could not possibly have been happier.

'I lay awake all night, listening to the old soldier's stertorous breathing, as he slept on his pallet by the side of her who had followed him to the ends of the earth, and I pondered on their strange, yet simple story; their happiness, so perfect, yet founded on so little.

'At sunrise I shook hands with the old couple and bade them farewell.'

The speaker was silent.

'You may say what you please,' one of the women exclaimed, 'her ideals were paltry. Her wants and desires were absurdly primitive. She was just a fool.'

'What did that matter?' replied another woman pensively. 'She was happy.'

On the horizon, Corsica was vanishing in the gloom of night, sinking slowly back into the sea, as if its vast shadowy form had manifested itself for no other purpose than to tell its tale of those two simple lovers who had found a refuge on its shores.

THE PHILOSOPHER
IN THE APPLE ORCHARD

Anthony Hope

It was a charmingly mild and balmy day. The sun shone beyond the orchard, and the shade was cool inside. A light breeze stirred the boughs of the old apple-tree under which the philosopher sat. None of these things did the philosopher notice, unless it might be when the wind blew about the leaves of the large volume on his knees, and he had to find his place again. Then he would exclaim against the wind, shuffle the leaves till he got the right page, and settle to his reading. The book was a treatise on ontology; it was written by another philosopher, a friend of this philosopher's; it bristled with fallacies, and this philosopher was discovering them all, and noting them on the fly-leaf at the end. He was not going to review the book (as some might have thought from his behaviour), or even to answer it in a work of his own. It was just that he found a pleasure in stripping any poor fallacy naked and crucifying it. Presently a girl in a white frock came into the orchard. She picked up an apple, bit it, and found it ripe. Holding it in her hand, she walked up to where the philosopher sat, and looked at him. He did not stir. She took a bite out of the apple, munched it, and swallowed it. The philosopher crucified a fallacy on the fly-leaf. The girl flung the apple away.

'Mr Jerningham,' said she, 'are you very busy?'

The philosopher, pencil in hand, looked up.

'No, Miss May,' said he, 'not very.'

'Because I want your opinion.'

'In one moment,' said the philosopher, apologetically.

He turned back to the fly-leaf and began to nail the last fallacy a little tighter to the cross. The girl regarded him, first with amused impatience, then with a vexed frown, finally with a wistful regret. He was so very old for his age, she thought; he could not be much beyond thirty; his hair was thick and full of waves, his eyes bright and clear, his complexion not yet divested of all youth's relics.

'Now, Miss May, I'm at your service,' said the philosopher, with a lingering look at his impaled fallacy; and he closed the book, keeping it, however, on his knee.

The girl sat down just opposite to him.

'It's a very important thing I want to ask you,' she began, tugging at a tuft of grass, 'and it's very—difficult, and you mustn't tell anyone I asked you; at least, I'd rather you didn't.'

'I shall not speak of it; indeed, I shall probably not remember it,' said the philosopher.

'And you mustn't look at me, please, while I'm asking you.'

'I don't think I was looking at you, but if I was I beg your pardon,' said the philosopher, apologetically.

She pulled the tuft of grass right out of the ground, and flung it from her with all her force.

'Suppose a man—' she began. 'No, that's not right.'

'You can take any hypothesis you please,' observed the

philosopher, 'but you must verify it afterward, of course.'

'Oh, do let me go on. Suppose a girl, Mr Jerningham—I wish you wouldn't nod.'

'It was only to show that I followed you.'

'Oh, of course you "follow me," as you call it. Suppose a girl had two lovers—you're nodding again—or, I ought to say, suppose there were two men who might be in love with a girl.'

'Only two?' asked the philosopher. 'You see, any number of men might be in love with—'

'Oh, we can leave the rest out,' said Miss May, with a sudden dimple; 'they don't matter.'

'Very well,' said the philosopher, 'if they are irrelevant we will put them aside.'

'Suppose, then, that one of these men was, oh, awfully in love with the girl, and—and proposed, you know—'

'A moment!' said the philosopher, opening a notebook. 'Let me take down his proposition. What was it?'

'Why, proposed to her—asked her to marry him,' said the girl, with a stare.

'Dear me! How stupid of me! I forgot that special use of the word. Yes?'

'The girl likes him pretty well, and her people approve of him, and all that, you know.'

'That simplifies the problem,' said the philosopher, nodding again.

'But she's not in—in love with him, you know. She doesn't really care for him—much. Do you understand?'

'Perfectly. It is a most natural state of mind.'

'Well then, suppose that there's another man—what are you writing?'

'I only put down (B)—like that,' pleaded the philosopher,

meekly exhibiting his notebook.

She looked at him in a sort of helpless exasperation, with just a smile somewhere in the background of it.

'Oh, you really are—' she exclaimed. 'But let me go on. The other man is a friend of the girl's: he's very clever—oh, fearfully clever—and he's rather handsome. You needn't put that down.'

'It is certainly not very material,' admitted the philosopher, and he crossed out 'handsome'; 'clever' he left.

'And the girl is most awfully—she admires him tremendously; she thinks him just the greatest man that ever lived, you know. And she—she—' The girl paused.

'I'm following,' said the philosopher, with pencil poised.

'She'd think it better than the whole world if—if she could be anything to him, you know.'

'You mean become his wife?'

'Well, of course I do—at least, I suppose I do.'

'You spoke rather vaguely, you know.'

The girl cast one glance at the philosopher as she replied: 'Well, yes; I did mean become his wife.'

'Yes. Well?'

'But,' continued the girl, starting on another tuft of grass, 'he doesn't think much about those things. He likes her. I think he likes her—'

'Well, doesn't dislike her?' suggested the philosopher. 'Shall we call him indifferent?'

'I don't know. Yes, rather indifferent. I don't think he thinks about it, you know. But she—she's pretty. You needn't put that down.'

'I was not about to do so,' observed the philosopher.

'She thinks life with him would be just heaven; and—and

she thinks she would make him awfully happy. She would—would be so proud of him, you see.'

'I see. Yes?'

'And—I don't know how to put it, quite—she thinks that if he ever thought about it at all he might care for her; because he doesn't care for anybody else, and she's pretty—'

'You said that before.'

'Oh dear, I dare say I did. And most men care for somebody, don't they? Some girl, I mean.'

'Most men, no doubt,' conceded the philosopher.

'Well then, what ought she to do? It's not a real thing, you know, Mr Jerningham. It's in—in a novel I was reading.' She said this hastily, and blushed as she spoke.

'Dear me! And it's quite an interesting case! Yes, I see. The question is, will she act most wisely in accepting the offer of the man who loves her exceedingly, but for whom she entertains only a moderate affection—'

'Yes; just a liking. He's just a friend.'

'Exactly. Or in marrying the other whom she loves ex—'

'That's not it. How can she marry him? He hasn't—he hasn't asked her, you see.'

'True; I forgot. Let us assume, though, for the moment, that he has asked her. She would then have to consider which marriage would probably be productive of the greater sum total of—'

'Oh, but you needn't consider that.'

'But it seems the best logical order. We can afterward make allowance for the element of uncertainty caused by—'

'Oh no; I don't want it like that. I know perfectly well which she'd do if he—the other man you know—asked her.'

'You apprehend that—'

'Never mind what I "apprehend". Take it as I told you.'
'Very good. A has asked her hand, B has not.'
'Yes.'
'May I take it that, but for the disturbing influence of B, A would be a satisfactory—er—candidate?'
'Ye—es; I think so.'
'She therefore enjoys a certainty of considerable happiness if she marries A?'
'Ye—es; not perfect, because of—B, you know.'
'Quite so, quite so; but still a fair amount of happiness. Is it not so?'
'I don't—well, perhaps.'
'On the other hand, if B did ask her, we are to postulate a higher degree of happiness for her?'
'Yes, please, Mr Jerningham—much higher.'
'For both of them?'
'For her. Never mind him.'
'Very well. That again simplifies the problem. But his asking her is a contingency only?'
'Yes, that's all.'
The philosopher spread out his hands.
'My dear young lady,' he said, 'it becomes a question of degree. How probable or improbable is it?'
'I don't know; not very probable—unless—'
'Well?'
'Unless he did happen to notice, you know.'
'Ah, yes; we supposed that, if he thought of it, he would probably take the desired step—at least, that he might be led to do so. Could she not—er—indicate her preference?'
'She might try—no, she couldn't do much. You see, he—he doesn't think about such things.'

'I understand precisely. And it seems to me, Miss May, that in that very fact we find our solution.'

'Do we?' she asked.

'I think so. He has evidently no natural inclination toward her—perhaps not toward marriage at all. Any feeling aroused in him would be necessarily shallow and, in a measure, artificial, and in all likelihood purely temporary. Moreover, if she took steps to arouse his attention one of two things would be likely to happen. Are you following me?'

'Yes, Mr Jerningham.'

'Either he would be repelled by her overtures, which you must admit is not improbable, and then the position would be unpleasant, and even degrading, for her; or, on the other hand, he might, through a misplaced feeling of gallantry—'

'Through what?'

'Through a mistaken idea of politeness, or a mistaken view of what was kind, allow himself to be drawn into a connection for which he had no genuine liking. You agree with me that one or other of these things would be likely?'

'Yes, I suppose they would, unless he did come to care for her.'

'Ah, you return to that hypothesis. I think it's an extremely fanciful one. No, she need not marry A; but she must let B alone.'

The philosopher closed his book, took off his glasses, wiped them, replaced them, and leaned back against the trunk of the apple-tree. The girl picked a dandelion in pieces. After a long pause she asked:

'You think B's feelings wouldn't be at all likely to—to change?'

'That depends on the sort of man he is. But if he is an

able man, with intellectual interests which engross him—a man who has chosen his path in life—a man to whom women's society is not a necessity—'

'He's just like that,' said the girl, and she bit the head off a daisy.

'Then,' said the philosopher, 'I see not the least reason for supposing that his feelings will change.'

'And would you advise her to marry the other—A?'

'Well, on the whole, I should. A is a good fellow (I think we made A a good fellow), he is a suitable match, his love for her is true and genuine—'

'It's tremendous!'

'Yes—and—er—extreme. She likes him. There is every reason to hope that her liking will develop into a sufficiently deep and stable affection. She will get rid of her folly about B, and make A a good wife. Yes, Miss May, if I were the author of your novel I should make her marry A, and I should call that a happy ending.'

A silence followed. It was broken by the philosopher.

'Is that all you wanted my opinion about, Miss May?' he asked, with his finger between the leaves of the treatise on ontology.

'Yes, I think so. I hope I haven't bored you?'

'I've enjoyed the discussion extremely. I had no idea that novels raised points of such psychological interest. I must find time to read one.'

The girl had shifted her position till, instead of her full face, her profile was turned toward him. Looking away toward the paddock that lay brilliant in sunshine on the skirts of the apple orchard, she asked in low slow tones, twisting her hands in her lap:

'Don't you think that perhaps if B found out afterward—when she had married A, you know—that she had cared for him so very, very much, he might be a little sorry?'

'If he were a gentleman he would regret it deeply.'

'I mean—sorry on his own account; that—that he had thrown away all that, you know?'

The philosopher looked meditative.

'I think,' he pronounced, 'that it is very possible he would. I can well imagine it.'

'He might never find anybody to love him like that again,' she said, gazing on the gleaming paddock.

'He probably would not,' agreed the philosopher.

'And—and most people like being loved, don't they?'

'To crave for love is an almost universal instinct, Miss May.'

'Yes, almost,' she said, with a dreary little smile. 'You see, he'll get old, and—and have no one to look after him.'

'He will.'

'And no home.'

'Well, in a sense, none,' corrected the philosopher, smiling. 'But really you'll frighten me. I'm a bachelor myself, you know, Miss May.'

'Yes,' she whispered, just audibly.

'And all your terrors are before me.'

'Well, unless—'

'Oh, we needn't have that "unless",' laughed the philosopher, cheerfully. 'There's no "unless" about it, Miss May.'

The girl jumped to her feet; for an instant she looked at the philosopher. She opened her lips as if to speak, and at the thought of what lay at her tongue's tip her face grew red. But the philosopher was gazing past her, and his eyes rested in calm contemplation on the gleaming paddock.

'A beautiful thing, sunshine, to be sure,' said he.

Her blush faded away into paleness; her lips closed. Without speaking, she turned and walked slowly away, her head drooping. The philosopher heard the rustle of her skirt in the long grass of the orchard; he watched her for a few moments.

'A pretty, graceful creature,' said he, with a smile. Then he opened his book, took his pencil in his hand, and slipped in a careful forefinger to mark the fly-leaf.

The sun had passed mid-heaven and began to decline westward before he finished the book. Then he stretched himself and looked at his watch.

'Good gracious, two o'clock! I shall be late for lunch!' and he hurried to his feet.

He was very late for lunch.

'Everything's cold,' wailed his hostess. 'Where have you been, Mr Jerningham?'

'Only in the orchard—reading.'

'And you've missed May!'

'Missed Miss May? How do you mean? I had a long talk with her this morning—a most interesting talk.'

'But you weren't here to say goodbye. Now you don't mean to say that you forgot that she was leaving by the two-o'clock train? What a man you are!'

'Dear me! To think of my forgetting it!' said the philosopher, shamefacedly.

'She told me to say goodbye to you for her.'

'She's very kind. I can't forgive myself.'

His hostess looked at him for a moment; then she sighed, and smiled, and sighed again.

'Have you everything you want?' she asked.

'Everything, thank you,' said he, sitting down opposite the cheese, and propping his book (he thought he would just run through the last chapter again) against the loaf; 'everything in the world that I want, thanks.'

His hostess did not tell him that the girl had come in from the apple orchard and run hastily upstairs, lest her friend should see what her friend did see in her eyes. So that he had no suspicion at all that he had received an offer of marriage—and refused it. And he did not refer to anything of that sort when he paused once in his reading and exclaimed:

'I'm really sorry I missed Miss May. That was an interesting case of hers. But I gave the right answer; the girl ought to marry A.'

And so the girl did.

THE LADY WITH THE DOG

Anton Chekhov

I

It was said that a new person had appeared on the seafront: a lady with a little dog. Dmitri Dmitritch Gurov, who had by then been a fortnight at Yalta, and so was fairly at home there, had begun to take an interest in new arrivals. Sitting in Verney's pavilion, he saw, walking on the seafront, a fair-haired young lady of medium height, wearing a béret; a white Pomeranian dog was running behind her.

And afterwards he met her in the public gardens and in the square several times a day. She was walking alone, always wearing the same béret, and always with the same white dog; no one knew who she was, and every one called her simply 'the lady with the dog'.

'If she is here alone without a husband or friends, it wouldn't be amiss to make her acquaintance,' Gurov reflected.

He was under forty, but he had a daughter already twelve years old, and two sons at school. He had been married young, when he was a student in his second year, and by now his wife seemed half as old again as he. She was a tall, erect woman with dark eyebrows, staid and dignified, and, as she said of herself, intellectual. She read a great deal, used phonetic spelling, called her husband, not Dmitri, but Dimitri, and he secretly considered her unintelligent, narrow, inelegant, was afraid of her, and did not like to be at home. He had begun being unfaithful to her long ago—had been unfaithful to her often, and, probably on that account, almost always spoke ill of women, and when they were talked about in his presence, used to call them 'the lower race'.

It seemed to him that he had been so schooled by bitter experience that he might call them what he liked, and yet he could not get on for two days together without 'the lower race'. In the society of men he was bored and not himself, with them he was cold and uncommunicative; but when he was in the company of women he felt free, and knew what to say to them and how to behave; and he was at ease with them even when he was silent. In his appearance, in his character, in his whole nature, there was something attractive and elusive which allured women and disposed them in his favour; he knew that, and some force seemed to draw him, too, to them.

Experience often repeated, truly bitter experience, had taught him long ago that with decent people, especially Moscow people—always slow to move and irresolute—every intimacy, which at first so agreeably diversifies life and appears a light and charming adventure, inevitably grows into a regular problem of extreme intricacy, and in the long run the situation becomes unbearable. But at every fresh meeting with an interesting woman this experience seemed to slip out of his memory, and he was eager for life, and everything seemed simple and amusing.

One evening he was dining in the gardens, and the lady in the béret came up slowly to take the next table. Her expression, her gait, her dress, and the way she did her hair told him that she was a lady, that she was married, that she was in Yalta for the first time and alone, and that she was dull here… The stories told of the immorality in such places as Yalta are to a great extent untrue; he despised them, and knew that such stories were for the most part made up by persons who would themselves have been glad to sin if they had been able; but when the lady sat down at the next table three paces from him, he remembered these tales of easy conquests, of trips to the mountains, and the tempting thought of a swift, fleeting love affair, a romance with an unknown woman, whose name he did not know, suddenly took possession of him.

He beckoned coaxingly to the Pomeranian, and when the dog came up to him he shook his finger at it. The Pomeranian growled: Gurov shook his finger at it again.

The lady looked at him and at once dropped her eyes.

'He doesn't bite,' she said, and blushed.

'May I give him a bone?' he asked; and when she nodded he asked courteously, 'Have you been long in Yalta?'

'Five days.'

'And I have already dragged out a fortnight here.'

There was a brief silence.

'Time goes fast, and yet it is so dull here!' she said, not looking at him.

'That's only the fashion to say it is dull here. A provincial will live in Belyov or Zhidra and not be dull, and when he comes here it's "Oh, the dullness! Oh, the dust!" One would think he came from Grenada.'

She laughed. Then both continued eating in silence, like strangers, but after dinner they walked side by side; and there sprang up between them the light jesting conversation of people who are free and satisfied, to whom it does not matter where they go or what they talk about. They walked and talked of the strange light on the sea: the water was of a soft warm lilac hue, and there was a golden streak from the moon upon it. They talked of how sultry it was after a hot day. Gurov told her that he came from Moscow, that he had taken his degree in Arts, but had a post in a bank; that he had trained as an opera-singer, but had given it up, that he owned two houses in Moscow... And from her he learnt that she had grown up in Petersburg, but had lived in S— since her marriage two years before, that she was staying another month in Yalta, and that her husband, who needed a holiday too, might perhaps come and fetch her. She was not sure whether her husband had a post in a Crown Department or under the Provincial Council—and was amused by her own ignorance. And Gurov learnt, too, that she was called Anna Sergeyevna.

Afterwards he thought about her in his room at the hotel—thought she would certainly meet him next day; it would be sure to happen. As he got into bed he thought how lately she had been a girl at school, doing lessons like his own daughter; he recalled the diffidence, the angularity, that was still manifest in her laugh and her manner of talking with a stranger. This must have been the first time in her life she had been alone in surroundings in which she was followed, looked at, and spoken to merely from a secret motive which she could hardly fail to guess. He recalled her slender, delicate neck, her lovely grey eyes.

'There's something pathetic about her, anyway,' he thought, and fell asleep.

II

A week had passed since they had made acquaintance. It was a holiday. It was sultry indoors, while in the street the wind whirled the dust round and round, and blew people's hats off. It was a thirsty day, and Gurov often went into the pavilion, and pressed Anna Sergeyevna to have syrup and water or an ice. One did not know what to do with oneself.

In the evening when the wind had dropped a little, they went out on the groyne to see the steamer come in. There were a great many people walking about the harbour; they had gathered to welcome someone, bringing bouquets. And two peculiarities of a well-dressed Yalta crowd were very conspicuous: the elderly ladies were dressed like young ones, and there were great numbers of generals.

Owing to the roughness of the sea, the steamer arrived late, after the sun had set, and it was a long time turning about before it reached the groyne. Anna Sergeyevna looked through her lorgnette at the steamer and the passengers as though looking for acquaintances, and when she turned to Gurov her eyes were shining. She talked a great deal and asked disconnected questions, forgetting next moment what she had asked; then she dropped her lorgnette in the crush.

The festive crowd began to disperse; it was too dark to see people's faces. The wind had completely dropped, but Gurov and Anna Sergeyevna still stood as though waiting to see someone else come from the steamer. Anna Sergeyevna was silent now, and sniffed the flowers without looking at Gurov.

'The weather is better this evening,' he said. 'Where shall we go now? Shall we drive somewhere?'

She made no answer.

Then he looked at her intently, and all at once put his arm round her and kissed her on the lips, and breathed in the moisture and the fragrance of the flowers; and he immediately looked round him, anxiously wondering whether anyone had seen them.

'Let us go to your hotel,' he said softly. And both walked quickly.

The room was close and smelt of the scent she had bought at the Japanese shop. Gurov looked at her and thought: 'What different people one meets in the world!' From the past he preserved memories of careless, good-natured women, who loved cheerfully and were grateful to him for the happiness he gave them, however brief it might be; and of women like his wife who loved without any genuine feeling, with superfluous phrases, affectedly, hysterically, with an expression that suggested that it was not love nor passion, but something more significant; and of two or three others, very beautiful, cold women, on whose faces he had caught a glimpse of a rapacious expression—an obstinate desire to snatch from life more than it could give, and these were capricious, unreflecting, domineering, unintelligent women not in their first youth, and when Gurov grew cold to them their beauty excited his hatred, and the lace on their linen seemed to him like scales.

But in this case there was still the diffidence, the angularity of inexperienced youth, an awkward feeling; and there was a sense of consternation as though someone had suddenly knocked at the door. The attitude of Anna Sergeyevna—'the lady with the dog'—to what had happened was somehow peculiar, very grave, as though it were her fall—so it seemed, and it was strange and inappropriate. Her face dropped and faded, and on both sides of it her long hair hung down mournfully; she mused in a dejected attitude like 'the woman who was a sinner' in an old-fashioned picture.

'It's wrong,' she said. 'You will be the first to despise me now.'

There was a watermelon on the table. Gurov cut himself a slice and began eating it without haste. There followed at least half an hour of silence.

Anna Sergeyevna was touching; there was about her the purity of a good, simple woman who had seen little of life. The solitary candle burning on the table threw a faint light on her face, yet it was clear that she was very unhappy.

'How could I despise you?' asked Gurov. 'You don't know what you are saying.'

'God forgive me,' she said, and her eyes filled with tears. 'It's awful.'

'You seem to feel you need to be forgiven.'

'Forgiven? No. I am a bad, low woman; I despise myself and don't attempt to justify myself. It's not my husband but myself I have deceived. And not only just now; I have been deceiving myself for a long time. My husband may be a good, honest man, but he is a flunkey! I don't know what he does there, what his work is, but I know he is a flunkey! I was twenty when I was married to him. I have been tormented by curiosity; I wanted something better. "There must be a different sort of life," I said to myself. I wanted to live! To live, to live! ...I was fired by curiosity...you don't understand it, but, I swear to God, I could not control myself; something happened to me: I could not be restrained. I told my husband I was ill, and came here... And here I have been walking about as though I were dazed, like a mad creature; ...and now I have become a vulgar, contemptible woman whom anyone may despise.'

Gurov felt bored already, listening to her. He was irritated by the naïve tone, by this remorse, so unexpected and inopportune; but for the tears in her eyes, he might have thought she was jesting or playing a part.

'I don't understand,' he said softly. 'What is it you want?'

She hid her face on his breast and pressed close to him.

'Believe me, believe me, I beseech you...' she said. 'I love a pure, honest life, and sin is loathsome to me. I don't know what I am doing. Simple people say: "The Evil One has beguiled me." And I may say of myself now that the Evil One has beguiled me.'

'Hush, hush!' he muttered.

He looked at her fixed, scared eyes, kissed her, talked softly and affectionately, and by degrees she was comforted, and her gaiety returned; they both began laughing.

Afterwards when they went out there was not a soul on the seafront. The town with its cypresses had quite a deathlike air, but the sea still broke noisily on the shore; a single barge was rocking on the waves, and a lantern was blinking sleepily on it.

They found a cab and drove to Oreanda.

'I found out your surname in the hall just now: it was written on the board—Von Diderits,' said Gurov. 'Is your husband a German?'

'No; I believe his grandfather was a German, but he is an Orthodox Russian himself.'

At Oreanda they sat on a seat not far from the church, looked down at the sea, and were silent. Yalta was hardly visible through the morning mist; white clouds stood motionless on the mountain-tops. The leaves did not stir on the trees, grasshoppers chirruped, and the monotonous hollow sound of the sea rising up from below, spoke of the peace, of the eternal sleep awaiting us. So it must have sounded when there was no Yalta, no Oreanda here; so it sounds now, and it will sound as indifferently and monotonously when we are all no more. And in this constancy, in this complete indifference to the life and death of each of us, there lies hid, perhaps, a pledge of our eternal salvation, of the unceasing movement of life upon earth, of unceasing progress towards perfection. Sitting beside a young woman who in the dawn seemed so lovely, soothed and spellbound in these magical surroundings—the sea, mountains, clouds, the open sky—Gurov thought how in reality everything is beautiful in this world when one reflects: everything except what we think or do ourselves when we forget our human dignity and the higher aims of our existence.

A man walked up to them—probably a keeper—looked at them and walked away. And this detail seemed mysterious and beautiful, too. They saw a steamer come from Theodosia, with its lights out in the glow of dawn.

'There is dew on the grass,' said Anna Sergeyevna, after a silence.

'Yes. It's time to go home.'

They went back to the town.

Then they met every day at twelve o'clock on the seafront, lunched and dined together, went for walks, admired the sea. She complained that she slept badly, that her heart throbbed violently; asked the same questions, troubled now by jealousy and now by the fear that he did not respect her sufficiently. And often in the square or gardens, when there was no one near them, he suddenly drew her to him and kissed her passionately. Complete idleness, these kisses in broad daylight while he looked round in dread of someone's seeing them, the heat, the smell of the sea, and the continual passing to and fro before him of idle, well-dressed, well-fed people, made a new man of him; he told Anna Sergeyevna how beautiful she was, how fascinating. He was impatiently passionate, he would not move a step away from her, while she was often pensive and continually urged him to confess that he did not respect her, did not love her in the least, and thought of her as nothing but a common woman. Rather late almost every evening they drove somewhere out of town, to Oreanda or to the waterfall; and the expedition was always a success, the scenery invariably impressed them as grand and beautiful.

They were expecting her husband to come, but a letter came from him, saying that there was something wrong with his eyes, and he entreated his wife to come home as quickly as possible. Anna Sergeyevna made haste to go.

'It's a good thing I am going away,' she said to Gurov. 'It's the finger of destiny!'

She went by coach and he went with her. They were driving the whole day. When she had got into a compartment of the express, and when the second bell had rung, she said:

'Let me look at you once more…look at you once again. That's right.'

She did not shed tears, but was so sad that she seemed ill, and her face was quivering.

'I shall remember you…think of you,' she said. 'God be with you; be happy. Don't remember evil against me. We are parting forever—it must be so, for we ought never to have met. Well, God be with you.'

The train moved off rapidly, its lights soon vanished from sight, and a minute later there was no sound of it, as though everything had conspired together to end as quickly as possible that sweet delirium, that madness. Left alone on the platform, and gazing into the dark distance, Gurov listened to the chirrup of the grasshoppers and the hum of the telegraph wires, feeling as though he had only just waked up. And he thought, musing, that there had been another episode or adventure in his life, and it, too, was at an end, and nothing was left of it but a memory... He was moved, sad, and conscious of a slight remorse. This young woman whom he would never meet again had not been happy with him; he was genuinely warm and affectionate with her, but yet in his manner, his tone, and his caresses there had been a shade of light irony, the coarse condescension of a happy man who was, besides, almost twice her age. All the time she had called him kind, exceptional, lofty; obviously he had seemed to her different from what he really was, so he had unintentionally deceived her....

Here at the station was already a scent of autumn; it was a cold evening.

'It's time for me to go north,' thought Gurov as he left the platform. 'High time!'

III

At home in Moscow everything was in its winter routine; the stoves were heated, and in the morning it was still dark when the children were having breakfast and getting ready for school, and the nurse would light the lamp for a short time. The frosts had begun already. When the first snow has fallen, on the first day of sledge-driving it is pleasant to see the white earth, the white roofs, to draw soft, delicious breath, and the season brings back the days of one's youth. The old limes and birches, white with hoar-frost, have a good-natured expression; they are nearer to one's heart than cypresses and palms, and near them one doesn't want to be thinking of the sea and the mountains.

Gurov was Moscow born; he arrived in Moscow on a fine frosty day, and when he put on his fur coat and warm gloves, and walked along Petrovka, and when on Saturday evening he heard the ringing of the bells, his recent trip and the places he had seen lost all charm for him. Little by little he became absorbed in Moscow life, greedily read three newspapers a day, and declared he did not read the Moscow papers on principle! He already felt a longing to go to restaurants, clubs, dinner-parties, anniversary celebrations, and he felt flattered at entertaining distinguished lawyers and artists, and at playing cards with a professor at the doctors' club. He could already eat a whole plateful of salt fish and cabbage.

In another month, he fancied, the image of Anna Sergeyevna would be shrouded in a mist in his memory, and only from time to time would visit him in his dreams with a touching smile as others did. But more than a month passed, real winter had come, and everything was still clear in his memory as though he had parted with Anna Sergeyevna only the day before. And his memories glowed more and more vividly. When in the evening stillness he heard from his study the voices of his children, preparing their lessons, or when he listened to a song or the organ at the restaurant, or the storm howled in the chimney, suddenly everything would rise up in his memory: what had happened on the groyne, and the early morning with the mist on the mountains, and the steamer coming from Theodosia, and the kisses. He would pace a long time about his room, remembering it all and smiling; then his memories passed into dreams, and in his fancy the past was mingled with what was to come. Anna Sergeyevna did not visit him in dreams, but followed him about everywhere like a shadow and haunted him. When he shut his eyes he saw her as though she were living before him, and she seemed to him lovelier, younger, tenderer than she was; and he imagined himself finer than he had been in Yalta. In the evenings she peeped out at him from the bookcase, from the fireplace, from the corner—he heard her breathing, the caressing rustle of her dress. In the street he watched the women, looking for someone like her.

He was tormented by an intense desire to confide his memories to someone. But in his home it was impossible to talk of his love, and he had no one outside; he could not talk to his tenants nor to anyone at the bank. And what had he to talk of? Had he been in love, then? Had there been anything beautiful, poetical, or edifying or simply interesting in his relations with Anna Sergeyevna? And there was nothing for him but to talk vaguely of love, of woman, and no one guessed what it meant; only his wife twitched her black eyebrows, and said:

'The part of a lady-killer does not suit you at all, Dimitri.'

One evening, coming out of the doctors' club with an official with whom he had been playing cards, he could not resist saying:

'If only you knew what a fascinating woman I made the acquaintance of in Yalta!'

The official got into his sledge and was driving away, but turned suddenly and shouted:

'Dmitri Dmitritch!'

'What?'

'You were right this evening: the sturgeon was a bit too strong!'

These words, so ordinary, for some reason moved Gurov to indignation, and struck him as degrading and unclean. What savage manners, what people! What senseless nights, what uninteresting, uneventful days! The rage for card-playing, the gluttony, the drunkenness, the continual talk always about the same thing. Useless pursuits and conversations always about the same things absorb the better part of one's time, the better part of one's strength, and in the end there is left a life grovelling and curtailed, worthless and trivial, and there is no escaping or getting away from it—just as though one were in a madhouse or a prison.

Gurov did not sleep all night, and was filled with indignation. And he had a headache all next day. And the next night he slept badly; he sat up in bed, thinking, or paced up and down his room. He was sick of his children, sick of the bank; he had no desire to go anywhere or to talk of anything.

In the holidays in December he prepared for a journey, and told his wife he was going to Petersburg to do something in the interests of a young friend—and he set off for S——. What for? He did not very well know himself. He wanted to see Anna Sergeyevna and to talk with her—to arrange a meeting, if possible.

He reached S——in the morning, and took the best room at the hotel, in which the floor was covered with grey army cloth, and on the table was an inkstand, grey with dust and adorned with a figure on horseback, with its hat in its hand and its head broken off. The hotel porter gave him the necessary information; Von Diderits lived in a house of his own in

Old Gontcharny Street—it was not far from the hotel: he was rich and lived in good style, and had his own horses; every one in the town knew him. The porter pronounced the name 'Dridirits'.

Gurov went without haste to Old Gontcharny Street and found the house. Just opposite the house stretched a long grey fence adorned with nails.

'One would run away from a fence like that,' thought Gurov, looking from the fence to the windows of the house and back again.

He considered: today was a holiday, and the husband would probably be at home. And in any case it would be tactless to go into the house and upset her. If he were to send her a note it might fall into her husband's hands, and then it might ruin everything. The best thing was to trust to chance. And he kept walking up and down the street by the fence, waiting for the chance. He saw a beggar go in at the gate and dogs fly at him; then an hour later he heard a piano, and the sounds were faint and indistinct. Probably it was Anna Sergeyevna playing. The front door suddenly opened, and an old woman came out, followed by the familiar white Pomeranian. Gurov was on the point of calling to the dog, but his heart began beating violently, and in his excitement he could not remember the dog's name.

He walked up and down, and loathed the grey fence more and more, and by now he thought irritably that Anna Sergeyevna had forgotten him, and was perhaps already amusing herself with someone else, and that that was very natural in a young woman who had nothing to look at from morning till night but that confounded fence. He went back to his hotel room and sat for a long while on the sofa, not knowing what to do, then he had dinner and a long nap.

'How stupid and worrying it is!' he thought when he woke and looked at the dark windows: it was already evening. 'Here I've had a good sleep for some reason. What shall I do in the night?'

He sat on the bed, which was covered by a cheap grey blanket, such as one sees in hospitals, and he taunted himself in his vexation:

'So much for the lady with the dog...so much for the adventure... You're in a nice fix...'

That morning at the station a poster in large letters had caught his eye. 'The Geisha' was to be performed for the first time. He thought of this and went to the theatre.

'It's quite possible she may go to the first performance,' he thought.

The theatre was full. As in all provincial theatres, there was a fog above the chandelier, the gallery was noisy and restless; in the front row the local dandies were standing up before the beginning of the performance, with their hands behind them; in the Governor's box the Governor's daughter, wearing a boa, was sitting in the front seat, while the Governor himself lurked modestly behind the curtain with only his hands visible; the orchestra was a long time tuning up; the stage curtain swayed. All the time the audience were coming in and taking their seats; Gurov looked at them eagerly.

Anna Sergeyevna, too, came in. She sat down in the third row, and when Gurov looked at her his heart contracted, and he understood clearly that for him there was in the whole world no creature so near, so precious, and so important to him; she, this little woman, in no way remarkable, lost in a provincial crowd, with a vulgar lorgnette in her hand, filled his whole life now, was his sorrow and his joy, the one happiness that he now desired for himself, and to the sounds of the inferior orchestra, of the wretched provincial violins, he thought how lovely she was. He thought and dreamed.

A young man with small side-whiskers, tall and stooping, came in with Anna Sergeyevna and sat down beside her; he bent his head at every step and seemed to be continually bowing. Most likely this was the husband whom at Yalta, in a rush of bitter feeling, she had called a flunkey. And there really was in his long figure, his side-whiskers, and the small bald patch on his head, something of the flunkey's obsequiousness; his smile was sugary, and in his buttonhole there was some badge of distinction like the number on a waiter.

During the first interval the husband went away to smoke; she remained alone in her stall. Gurov, who was sitting in the stalls, too, went up to her and said in a trembling voice, with a forced smile:

'Good-evening.'

She glanced at him and turned pale, then glanced again with horror, unable to believe her eyes, and tightly gripped the fan and the lorgnette in her hands, evidently struggling with herself not to faint. Both were silent. She was sitting, he was standing, frightened by her confusion and not venturing to sit down beside her. The violins and the flute began tuning up. He felt suddenly frightened; it seemed as though all the people in the boxes were looking at them. She got up and went quickly to the door; he followed her, and both walked senselessly along passages, and up and down stairs, and figures in legal, scholastic, and civil service uniforms, all wearing badges, flitted before their eyes. They caught glimpses of ladies, of fur coats hanging on pegs; the draughts blew on them, bringing a smell of stale tobacco. And Gurov, whose heart was beating violently, thought:

'Oh, heavens! Why are these people here and this orchestra!...'

And at that instant he recalled how when he had seen Anna Sergeyevna off at the station he had thought that everything was over and they would never meet again. But how far they were still from the end!

On the narrow, gloomy staircase over which was written 'To the Amphitheatre,' she stopped.

'How you have frightened me!' she said, breathing hard, still pale and overwhelmed. 'Oh, how you have frightened me! I am half dead. Why have you come? Why?'

'But do understand, Anna, do understand...' he said hastily in a low voice. 'I entreat you to understand...'

She looked at him with dread, with entreaty, with love; she looked at him intently, to keep his features more distinctly in her memory.

'I am so unhappy,' she went on, not heeding him. 'I have thought of nothing but you all the time; I live only in the thought of you. And I wanted to forget, to forget you; but why, oh, why, have you come?'

On the landing above them two schoolboys were smoking and looking down, but that was nothing to Gurov; he drew Anna Sergeyevna to him, and began kissing her face, her cheeks, and her hands.

'What are you doing, what are you doing!' she cried in horror, pushing him away. 'We are mad. Go away today; go away at once... I beseech you by all that is sacred, I implore you... There are people coming this way!'

Someone was coming up the stairs.

'You must go away,' Anna Sergeyevna went on in a whisper. 'Do you hear, Dmitri Dmitritch? I will come and see you in Moscow. I have never been happy; I am miserable now, and I never, never shall be happy, never! Don't make me suffer still more! I swear I'll come to Moscow. But now let us part. My precious, good, dear one, we must part!'

She pressed his hand and began rapidly going downstairs, looking round at him, and from her eyes he could see that she really was unhappy. Gurov stood for a little while, listened, then, when all sound had died away, he found his coat and left the theatre.

IV

And Anna Sergeyevna began coming to see him in Moscow. Once in two or three months she left S——, telling her husband that she was going to consult a doctor about an internal complaint—and her husband believed her, and did not believe her. In Moscow she stayed at the Slaviansky Bazaar hotel, and at once sent a man in a red cap to Gurov. Gurov went to see her, and no one in Moscow knew of it.

Once he was going to see her in this way on a winter morning (the messenger had come the evening before when he was out). With him walked his daughter, whom he wanted to take to school: it was on the way. Snow was falling in big wet flakes.

'It's three degrees above freezing-point, and yet it is snowing,' said Gurov to his daughter. 'The thaw is only on the surface of the earth; there is quite a different temperature at a greater height in the atmosphere.'

'And why are there no thunderstorms in the winter, father?'

He explained that, too. He talked, thinking all the while that he was going to see her, and no living soul knew of it, and probably never would know. He had two lives: one, open, seen and known by all who cared to know, full of relative truth and of relative falsehood, exactly like the lives of his friends and acquaintances; and another life running its course in secret. And through some strange, perhaps accidental, conjunction of circumstances, everything that was essential, of interest and of value to him, everything in which he was sincere and did not deceive himself, everything that made the kernel of his life, was hidden from other people; and all that was false in him, the sheath in which he hid himself to conceal the truth—such, for instance, as his work in the bank, his discussions at the club, his 'lower race,' his presence with his wife at anniversary festivities—all that was open. And he judged of others by himself, not believing in what he saw, and always believing that every man had his real, most interesting life under the cover of secrecy and under the cover of night. All personal life rested on secrecy, and possibly it was partly on that account that civilized man was so nervously anxious that personal privacy should be respected.

After leaving his daughter at school, Gurov went on to the Slaviansky Bazaar. He took off his fur coat below, went upstairs, and softly knocked at the door. Anna Sergeyevna, wearing his favourite grey dress, exhausted by the journey and the suspense, had been expecting him since the evening before. She was pale; she looked at him, and did not smile, and he had hardly come in when she fell on his breast. Their kiss was slow and prolonged, as though they had not met for two years.

'Well, how are you getting on there?' he asked. 'What news?'

'Wait; I'll tell you directly... I can't talk.'

She could not speak; she was crying. She turned away from him, and pressed her handkerchief to her eyes.

'Let her have her cry out. I'll sit down and wait,' he thought, and he sat down in an armchair.

Then he rang and asked for tea to be brought to him, and while he drank his tea she remained standing at the window with her back to him. She was crying from emotion, from the miserable consciousness that their life was so hard for them; they could only meet in secret, hiding themselves from people, like thieves! Was not their life shattered?

'Come, do stop!' he said.

It was evident to him that this love of theirs would not soon be over, that he could not see the end of it. Anna Sergeyevna grew more and more attached to him. She adored him, and it was unthinkable to say to her that it was bound to have an end some day; besides, she would not have believed it!

He went up to her and took her by the shoulders to say something affectionate and cheering, and at that moment he saw himself in the looking-glass.

His hair was already beginning to turn grey. And it seemed strange to him that he had grown so much older, so much plainer during the last few years. The shoulders on which his hands rested were warm and quivering. He felt compassion for this life, still so warm and lovely, but probably already not far from beginning to fade and wither like his own. Why did she love him so much? He always seemed to women different from what he was, and they loved in him not himself, but the man created by their imagination, whom they had been eagerly seeking all their lives; and afterwards, when they noticed their mistake, they loved him all the same. And not one of them had been happy with him. Time passed, he had made their acquaintance, got on with them, parted, but he had never once loved; it was anything you like, but not love.

And only now when his head was grey he had fallen properly, really in love—for the first time in his life.

Anna Sergeyevna and he loved each other like people very close and akin, like husband and wife, like tender friends; it seemed to them that fate itself had meant them for one another, and they could not understand why he had a wife and she a husband; and it was as though they were a pair of birds of passage, caught and forced to live in different cages. They forgave each other for what they were ashamed of in their past, they forgave everything in the present, and felt that this love of theirs had changed them both.

In moments of depression in the past he had comforted himself with any arguments that came into his mind, but now he no longer cared for arguments; he felt profound compassion, he wanted to be sincere and tender…

'Don't cry, my darling,' he said. 'You've had your cry; that's enough… Let us talk now, let us think of some plan.'

Then they spent a long while taking counsel together, talked of how to avoid the necessity for secrecy, for deception, for living in different towns and not seeing each other for long at a time. How could they be free from this intolerable bondage?

'How? How?' he asked, clutching his head. 'How?'

And it seemed as though in a little while the solution would be found, and then a new and splendid life would begin; and it was clear to both of them that they had still a long, long road before them, and that the most complicated and difficult part of it was only just beginning.

MARU

Henry de Vere Stacpoole

The night was filled with vanilla and frangipani odours, and the endless sound of the rollers on the reef. Somewhere away back amidst the trees a woman was singing; the tide was out, and from the verandah of Lygon's house, across the star-shot waters of the lagoon, moving yellow points of light caught the eye. They were spearing fish by torchlight in the reef pools.

It had been a shell lagoon once, and in the old days, men had come to Tokahoe for sandalwood; now there was only copra to be had, and just enough for one man to deal with. Tokahoe is only a little island, where one cannot make a fortune, but where you may live fortunately enough if your tastes are simple and beyond the lure of whisky and civilization.

The last trader had died in this paradise of whisky—or gin—I forget which, and his ghost was supposed to walk the beach on moonlit nights, and it was apropos of this that Lygon suddenly put the question to me, 'Do you believe in ghosts?'

'Do you?' replied I.

'I don't know,' said Lygon. 'I almost think I do, because everyone does. Oh, I know a handful of hardheaded super-civilized people say they don't, but the mass of humanity does. The Polynesians and Micronesians do; go to Japan, go to Ireland, go anywhere and everywhere you will find ghost believers.'

'Lombroso has written something like that,' said I.

'Has he? Well, it's a fact, but all the same, it's not evidence; the universality of a belief seems to hint at reality in the thing believed in—yet what is more wanting in real reason than Tabu? Yet Tabu is universal. You find men here who daren't touch an arm tree because arm trees are Tabu to them; or cat turtle or touch a dead body. Well, look at the Jews; a dead body is Tabu to a Cohen; India is riddled with the business, so's English Society—it's all the same thing under different disguises.

'Funny that talking of ghosts we should have touched on this, for when I asked you, did you believe in ghosts, I had a ghost story in mind, and Tabu comes into it. This is it.'

And this is the story somewhat as told by Lygon:

Some fifty years back, when Pease was in a pirate hold, and Hayes in his bloom, and the top-sails of the *Leonora* a terror to all dusky beholders, Mara was a young man of twenty. He was son of Malemake, King of Fukariva, a kingdom the size of a soup plate, nearly as round and without its middle; an atoll island, in short; just a ring of coral, sea beaten and circling, like a bezel, its sapphire lagoon.

Fukariva lies in the Paumotus or Dangerous Archipelago, where the currents run every way, and the winds are unaccountable. The underwriters to this day fight shy of its Paumotus trader, and in the 1860s few ships came here, and the few that came were on questionable business. Maru, up to the time he was twenty years of age, only remembered three.

There was the Spanish ship that came into the lagoon when he was only seven. The picture of her remained with him, burning and brilliant, yet tinged with the atmosphere of nightmare; its big top-sail schooner, that lay for a week mirroring herself on the lagoon water whilst she refitted; fellows with red handkerchiefs tied round their heads crawling aloft, and laying out the spars. They came ashore for water, and what they could find in the way of taro and nuts, and made hay on the beach, insulting the island women till the men drove them off. Then, when she was clearing the lagoon, its brass gun was run out and fired, leaving a score of dead and wounded on that salt white beach.

That was the Spaniard. Then came a whaler, who took what she wanted, and cut down trees for fuel and departed, leaving behind the smell of her as an enduring recollection; and lastly, when Maru was about eighteen, a little old schooner slank in one early morning.

She lay in the lagoon like a mangy dog, a humble ship, very unlike the Spaniard or the blustering whale-man; she only wanted water and a few vegetables, and her men gave no trouble; then, one evening, she slank out again with the ebb, but she left something behind her—smallpox. It cleared the island, and of the 150 subjects of King Malemake, only ten were left—twelve people in all, counting the king and Maru.

The king died of a broken heart and age, and of the eleven people left, three were women, widows of men who had died of the smallpox.

Maru was unmarried, and as king (of the Community) he might have collected the women for his own household.

But he had no thought of anything but grief; grief for his father and the people who were gone. He drew apart from the others, and the seven widowers began to arrange matters as to the distribution of the three widows. They began with arguments and ended with clubs; three men were killed, and one of the women killed another man because he had brained the man of her fancy.

Then the dead were buried in the lagoon—Maru refusing to help because of his Tabu—and the three newly-married couples settled down to live their lives, leaving Maru out in the cold. He was no longer the king. The women despised him because he hadn't fought for one of them, and the men because he had failed in brutality and leadership. They were a hard lot, true survivors of the fittest, and Maru, straight as a palm tree, dark-eyed, gentle, and a dreamer, seemed, amongst them, like a man of another tribe and time.

He lived alone, and sometimes in the sun blaze on that great ring of coral, he fancied he saw the spirits of the departed walking as they had walked in life, and sometimes it might be thought he heard the voice of his father chiding him.

When the old man died Maru had refused to touch the body or help in its burial. Filial love, his own salvation, nothing would have induced Maru to break his Tabu, which barred him from touching a dead body.

It was part of him, an iron reef in his character beyond the influence of will.

II

One morning, some six weeks after all this marrying and settling down, a brig came into the lagoon. She was a Blackbirder, the *Portsoy*, owned and captained by Colin Robertson, a Banffshire man, hence the name of his brig. Robertson and his men landed, took off water, coconuts, bananas, and everything else they could find worth taking. Then they turned their attention to the population. Four men were not a great find, but Robertson was not above trifles; he recruited them; that is to say, he kicked them into his boat and took them on board the *Portsoy*, leaving the three widows, grass widows now—wailing on the shore. He had no finer feelings about the marriage tie, and he reckoned they would make out somehow. They were no use to him as labour, and they were ill-favoured; all the same, being a man of gallantry and some humour, he dipped his flag to them as the *Portsoy* cleared the lagoon and breasted the tumble at the break.

Maru, standing aft, saw the island with the white foam fighting the coral and the gulls threshing around the break; saw the palms cut against the pale aquamarine of the skyline that swept up into the burning blue of noon; heard the long rumble and boom of the surf on the following wind, and watched and listened till the sound of the surf died to nothingness, and of the island nothing remained but the palm tops, like pin-heads above the sea dazzle.

He felt no grief. But there came to him a new and strange thing, a silence, that the ship-board sounds could not break. Since birth the eternal boom of the waves on coral had been in his ears, night and day, and day and night, louder in storms, but always there. It was gone. That was why, despite the sound of the bow wash, and boost of the waves, and the creak of cordage and block, the brig seemed to have carried

Maru into the silence of a new world.

He worked free of the Paumotus into the region of settled winds and accountable currents passing atolls, and reefs that showed like the threshing of a shark's tail in the blue, heading north-west in a world of wind and waves and sky, desolate of life, and, for Maru, the land of Nowhere.

So it went on from week to week, and, as far as he was concerned, so it might have gone on forever. He knew nothing of the world into which he had been suddenly snatched, and land, which was not a ring of coral surrounding a lagoon, was for him unthinkable.

He knew nothing of navigation, and the brass-bound wheel, at which a sailor was always standing with his hands on the spokes, now twirling it this way, now that, had for him a fascination beyond words, the fascination of a strange toy for a little child, and something more. It was the first wheel he had ever seen, and its movements about its axis seemed magical, and it was never left without someone to hold it and move it—why? The mystery of the binnacle into which the wheel-mover was always staring, as a man stares into a rock pool after fish, was almost as fascinating.

Maru peeped into the binnacle one day, and saw the fish, something like a star fish, that still moved and trembled. Then someone kicked him away, and he ran forward and hid, feeling that he had pried into the secrets of the white men's gods, and fearing the consequences.

But the white men's gods were not confined to the wheel and binnacle; down below they had a god that could warn them of the weather, for that day at noon, and for no apparent reason, the sailors began to strip the brig of her canvas. Then the sea rose, and two hours later the cyclone seized them.

It blew everything away, and then took them into its calm heart, where, dancing like giants in dead still air, and with the sea for a ballroom floor, the hundred-foot-high waves broke the Portnoy to pieces.

Maru alone was saved, clinging to a piece of hatch cover, half-stunned, confused, yet unafraid and feeling vaguely that the magic wheel and little trembling fish god had somehow betrayed the white men. He knew that he was not to die, because this strange world that had taken him from his island had not done with him yet, and the sea, in touch with him like this and half-washing over him at times, had no terror for him, for he had learned to swim before he had learned to walk. Also his stomach was full; he had been eating biscuits whilst the *Portsoy's* canvas was being stripped away, and though the wind was strong enough almost to whip the food from his hands.

The peaceful swell that followed the cyclone was a thing enough to have driven an ordinary man mad with terror. Now lifted hill-high on a glassy slope, the whole wheel of the horizon came to view under the blowing wind and blazing sun, then gently down—sliding, the hatch cover would sink to a valley-bottom only to climb again a glassy slope, and rise again into the wind and sun. Foam flecks passed on the surface, and in the green sun-dazzled crystal of the valley floors, he glimpsed strips of fucus floating far down, torn by the storm from their rock attachments, and through the sloping wall of glass, up which the hatch cover was climbing, he once glimpsed a shark, lifted and cradled in it ridge of the great swell, strange to see as a fly in amber or a fish in ice.

The hatch cover was sweeping with a four-knot current, moving with a whole world of things concealed, or half-seen or hinted at. A sea current is a street; it is more, it is a moving pavement for the people of the sea; jelly fish were being carried with Maru on the great swell running with the current, a turtle broke the water close to him and plunged again, and once in a while roaring reef passed by only a few cable lengths away. He could see the rock exposed for a moment, and the water closing on it in a tumble of foam.

III

For a day and a night and a day and a night the voyage continued, the swell falling to a gentle heave, and then in the dawn came a sail, the mat-sail of a canoe like a brown wing cut against the haliotis-shell coloured sky.

In the canoe was a girl, naked as the new moon. Paddle in hand, and half-crouching, she drove the canoe towards him, the sail loose and flapping in the wind. Then he was on board the canoe, but how he got there he scarcely knew; the whole thing was like a dream within a dream.

In the canoe there was nothing, neither food nor water, only some fishing lines, and as he lay exhausted, consumed with thirst and faint with hunger, he saw the girl resetting the sail. She had been fishing last evening from an island up north, and blown out to sea by a squall, had failed to make the land again, but she had sighted an island in the south-west, and was making for it, when she saw the hatch cover and the brown, clinging form of Maru.

As he lay half-dead in the bottom of the canoe, he watched her as she crouched with eyes fixed on the island and the steering paddle in hand, but before they could reach it, a squall took them, half-filling the canoe with rain-water, and Maru drank and drank till his ribs stood out, and then, renewed, half-rose, as the canoe, steered by the girl, rushed past tumbling green seas and a broken reef to a beach white as salt, towards which the great trees came down with the bread-fruits dripping with the new-fallen rain, and the palms bending like whips in the wind.

IV

Talia, that was her name, and though her language was different from the tongue of Maru, it had a likeness of a sort. In those days that little island was uncharted and entirely desolate but for the gulls of the reef and the birds of the woods, and it was a wonderland to Maru, whose idea of land as a sea-beaten ring of coral was shattered by woods that bloomed green as a sea-cave to the moonlight, high ground, where rivulets danced amidst the ferns, and a beach protected from the outer seas by a far-flung line of reefs. Talia to him was as wonderful as the island; she had come to him out of the sea; she had saved his life; she was as different from the women of the Paumotus as day from night. A European would have called her beautiful, but Maru had no thought of her beauty or her sex; she was just a being, beneficent, almost divorced from earth; the strangest thing in the strange world that Fate had seized him into, part with the great heaving swell he had ridden so long, the turtle that had broken up to look at him, the spouting reef, the sunsets over wastes of water, and the stars spread over wastes of sky.

He worshipped her in his way, and he might have worshipped her at a greater distance, only for the common bond of youth between them, and the incessant call of the world around them. Talia was practical; she seemed to have forgotten her people, and that island up north, and to live entirely in the moment. They made two shacks in the bushes, and she taught him island woodcraft, and the uses of berries and fruit that he had never seen before; also when to fish in the lagoon; for a month after they reached the island the poisonous season arrived, and Talia knew it, how, who can tell? She knew many things by instinct, the approach of storms, and when the poisonous season had passed, the times for fishing, and little by little their tongues, that had almost been divided at first, became almost one so that they could chatter together on all sorts of things, and she could tell him that her name was Talia, the daughter of Tepairu, that her island was named Makea, that her people had twenty canoes, big ones, and many little ones, and that Tepairu was not the name of a man, but a woman. That Tepairu was queen or chief woman of her people, now that her husband was dead.

And Maru was able to tell her by degrees of what he would remember, of the old Spanish ship, and how she spouted smoke and thunder, and killed the beach people, of his island and its shape—he drew it on the sand, and Talia, who knew nothing of atolls, at first refused to believe in it, thinking he was jesting—of his father, who was chief man or king of Fukariva, and of the destruction of the tribe. Then he told of the ship with the little wheel—he drew it on the sand—and the little fish god; of the centre of the cyclone, where the waves were like white dancing men, and of his journey on the hatch cover across the blue heaving sea.

They would swim in the lagoon together, right out to the reefs where the great rollers were always breaking, and out there Talia always seemed to remember her island, pointing north with her eyes fixed across the sea dazzle, as though she could see it, and her people, and the twenty canoes beached on the spume white beach beneath the palms.

'Some day they will come,' said Talia. She knew her people, those sea rovers, inconsequent as the gulls. Some day, for some reason or none, one of the fishing canoes would fish as far as this island, or be blown there by some squall. She would take Maru back with her. She told him this.

The thought began to trouble Maru. Then he grew gloomy. He was in love. Love had hit him suddenly. Somehow, and in some mysterious manner, she had changed from a beneficent being, and part of a dream, to a girl of flesh and blood. She knew it, and at the same moment he turned for her into a man.

Up to this she had no thought of him except as an individual, for all her dreams about him, he might as well have been a palm-tree, but now it was different, and in a flash he was everything. The surf on the reef said, Maru, and the wind in the trees, Maru, and the gulls fishing and crying at the break had one word, Maru! Maru! Maru!

Then, one day, swimming out near the bigger break in the reefs, a current drove them together, their shoulders touched, and Maru's arm went round her, and amidst the blue laughing sea and the shouting of the gulls, he told her that the whole world was Talia, and as he told her and as she listened, the current of the ebb, like a treacherous hand, was drawing them through the break towards the devouring sea.

They had to fight their way back, the ebb just beginning would soon be a mill-race, and they knew, and neither could help the other. It was a hard struggle for love and life against the enmity against life and love that hides in all things from the heart of man to the heart of the sea, but they won. They had reached calm waters, and were within twenty strokes of the beach when Talia cried out suddenly and sank.

Maru, who was slightly in front, turned and found her gone; she had been seized with cramp, the cramp that comes from over-exertion, but he did not know that; the lagoon was free of sharks, but, despite that fact, and the fact he did not fear them, he fancied for one fearful moment that a shark had taken her.

Then he saw her below, a dusky form on the coral floor, and he dived.

He brought her to the surface, reached the sandy beach, and, carrying her in his arms, ran with her to the higher level of the sands, and placed her beneath the shade of the trees. She moved in his arms as he carried her, and when he laid her down, her breast heaved in one great sigh, water ran from her mouth, her limbs stiffened, and she moved no more.

Then all the world became black for Maru; he knew nothing of the art of resuscitating the drowned. Talia was dead.

He ran amongst the trees crying out that Talia was dead; he struck himself against tree boles and was tripped by ground lianas; the things of the forest seemed trying to kill him too. Then he hid amongst the ferns, lying on his face, and telling the earth that Talia was dead. Then came sundown, and after that the green moonlight of the woods, and suddenly sleep, with a vision of blue laughing sea and Talia swimming beside him, and then day again, and with the day the vision of Talia lying dead beneath the trees. He could not bury her. He could not touch her. The iron reef of his Tabu held firm, indestructible, unalterable as the main currents of the sea.

He picked fruits and ate them like an animal, and without knowing that he ate, torn towards the beach by the passionate desire to embrace once more the form that he loved, but held from the act by a grip ten thousand years old, and immutable as gravity or the spirit that lives in religions.

He must not handle the dead. Through all his grief came a weird touch of comfort; she had not been dead when he carried her ashore. He had not touched the dead.

Then terrible thoughts came to him of what would happen to Talia if he left her lying there. Of what predatory gulls might do. He had some knowledge of these matters, and past visions of what had happened on Fukariva, when the dead were too numerous for burial, came to him, making him shiver like a whipped dog. He could, at all events, drive the birds away, without touching her, without even looking at her, his presence on the beach would keep the birds away. It was near noon when this thought came to him. He had been lying on the ground, but he sat up now as though listening to this thought. Then he rose up and came along cautiously amongst the trees. As he came, the rumble of the reef grew louder, and the seawind began to reach him through the leaves; then the light of day grew stronger, and slipping between the palm boles, he pushed a great bread-fruit leaf aside and peeped, and there, on the blinding beach, under, the forenoon sun, more clearly even than he had seen the ghosts of men on Fukariva, he saw the ghost of Talia walking by the sea and wringing its hands.

Then the forest took him again, mad, this time, with terror.

When on Fukariva he had seen the ghosts of men walking in the sun-blaze on the coral, he had felt no terror; he had never seen them except on waking from sleep beneath some tree, and the sight of them had never lasted for more than a moment. He had said to himself, 'They are the spirits of the departed,' and they had seemed to him part of the scheme of things, like reflections cast on the lagoon, or the spirit voices heard in the wind, or dreams, or the ships that had come from Nowhere and departed Nowhere.

But the ghost of Talia was different from these. It was in some tremendous way real, and it wept because the body of Talia lay unburied.

He had made it weep.

He alone could give it rest.

Away, deep in the woods, hiding amongst the bushes, springing alive with alarm at the slightest sound, he debated this matter with himself, and curiously, now, love did not move him at all or urge him; it was as though the ghost of Talia had stepped between him and his love for Talia, not destroying it, but obscuring it. Talia for him had become two things: the body he had left lying on the sand under the trees, and the ghost he had seen walking on the beach; the real Talia no longer existed for him, except as the vaguest wraith. He lay in the bushes, facing the fact that so long as the body lay unburied the ghost would walk. It might even leave the beach and come to him.

This thought brought him from his hiding-place; he could not be alone with it amongst the bushes, and then he found that he could not stand alone with it amongst the trees, for at any moment she might appear, wringing her hands, in one of the glades, or glide to his side from behind one of the tree boles.

He made for the southern beach.

Although unused to woods, till he reached this island he had the instinct for direction, a brain compass more mysterious than the little trembling fish that had directed the movements of the wheel on board the *Portsoy*. Making due south, amidst the gloom of the trees, he reached the beach where the sun was blazing on the sands and the birds flying and calling over the lagoon. The reef lay far out, a continuous line, unlike the reefs to the north, continuous but for a single break through which the last of the ebb was flowing out oilily, mirroring a palm-tree that stood there like the warden of the lagoon. The sound of the surf was low, the wind had died away, and as Maru stood watching and listening, peace came to his distracted soul.

He felt safe here. Even when Talia had been with him the woods had always seemed to him peopled with lurking things, unused as he was to trees in great masses; and now released from them and touched again by the warmth of the sun he felt safe. It seemed to him that the ghost could not come here. The gulls said it to him and the flashing water, and as he lay down on the sands, the surf on the reef said it to him. It was too far away for the ghost to come. It seemed to him that he had travelled many thousand miles from a country remote as his extreme youth, losing everything on the way but a weariness greater than time could hold or thought take recognition of.

Then he fell asleep and he slept whilst the sun went down into the west and the flood swept into the lagoon and the stars broke out above. That tremendous sleep unstirred by the vaguest dream lasted till the dawn was full.

Then he sat up, renewed as though God had remade him in mind and body.

A gull was strutting on the sands by the water's edge, its long shadow strutting after it, and the shadow of the gull flew straight as a javelin into the renewed mind of Maru. Talia was not dead. He had not seen her ghost. She had come to life and had been walking by the sea wringing her hands for him thinking him drowned. For the form he had seen walking in the sands had cast a shadow. He remembered that now. Ghosts do not cast shadows.

And instantly his mind, made reasonable by rest and sleep, revisualized the picture that had terrified his mind distraught by grief. That was a real form, what folly could have made him doubt it? Talia was alive—alive, warm, and waiting for him on the northern beach, and seized him with a great joy that made him shout aloud as he sprang to his feet yet with a pain at his heart like the pain of a rankling spearwound as he broke through the trees shouting as he ran: 'Talia! Talia! Talia!'

He passed the bushes where he had hidden, and the ferns. He heard the sounds of the surf coming to meet him, he saw the veils of the northern sands and lagoon and sea.

He stood and looked.

Nothing.

He ran to the place where he had laid her beneath the trees, there was still faintly visible the slight depression made by her body, and close by, strangely and clearly cut, the imprint of a little foot.

Nothing else.

He stood and called and called, and no answer came but the wood echo and the sound of the morning wind; then he ran to the sea edge. Then he knew.

The sand was trodden up and on the sand, clear cut and fresh, lay the mark left by a beached canoe and the marks left by the feet of the men who had beached her and floated her again.

They had come—perhaps her own people—came, maybe, yesterday whilst he was hiding from his fears, debating with his Tabu—came, and found her, and taken her away.

He plunged into the lagoon and, swimming like an otter and helped by the out-going tide, reached the reef. Scrambling on to the rough coral, bleeding from cuts but feeling nothing of his wounds, he stood with wrinkled eyes facing the sea blaze and with the land-breeze blowing past him out beyond the thundering foam of the reef to the blue and heaving sea.

Away to the north, like a brown wing-tip, showed the sail of a canoe. He watched it. Tossed by the lilt of the swell it seemed beckoning to him. Now it vanished in the sea dazzle, now reappeared, dwindling to a point, to vanish at last like a dream of the sea, gone, never to be recaptured.

'And Maru?' I asked of Lygon, 'Did he ever—'

'Never,' said Lygon. 'The islands of the sea are many. Wait.' He struck a gong that stood close to his chair, struck it three times, and the sounds passing into the night mixed with the voices of the canoe men returning from fishing on the reef.

Then a servant came on to the verandah, an old, old man, half-bent like a withered tree.

'Maru,' said Lygon, 'you can take away these glasses—but one moment, Maru, tell this gentleman your story.'

'The islands of the sea are many,' said Maru, like a child repeating its lesson. He paused for a moment as though trying to remember some more, then he passed out of the lamplight with the glasses.

'A year ago he remembered the whole story,' said Lygon.

But for me the whole story lay in those words, that voice, those trembling hands that seemed still searching for what the eyes could see no more.

MARY ANSELL

Martin Armstrong

Mary Brakefield, wife of Samuel Brakefield, landlord of the Golden Lion, Netherhinton, made her way along the accustomed hedge-bordered road that led to the foot of the downs. From the road end the coarse grass of the downs rose in a single abrupt slope to the flat summit, which was enclosed by a great rampart rising nobly from its broad ditch.

The face of this ancient earthwork was so steep that he who climbed it could do so only on his knees, pulling himself up with his hands by the strong tufted grass that clothed it like a shaggy fur. Every Thursday Mary Brakefield took the same walk, and always alone. She was a quiet, kindly, respectable woman, not otherwise eccentric, and her husband and the neighbours, though they themselves never took a walk except when some definite object required, had long since grown so accustomed to this weekly stroll of hers that they had ceased to regard it as strange, even when the weather was so stormy that it was incredible that anyone should walk out, much less climb the bare downs, for mere pleasure.

On winter evenings, when, looking from their cottage

windows into a stormy twilight, the villagers saw a lonely figure struggling against the wind and rain down the long village street, they would say without surprise: 'It'll only be Mrs Brakefield coming back from her walk.'

She was a spare, neat woman of forty, though strangers put her age down at over fifty. Her face was pale and bony; the eyes, too, were pale and weary and red-rimmed; and the corners of her mouth had a bitter downward droop that on rare occasions vanished suddenly and surprisingly into a charming, wistful smile.

It was the beginning of October, and the hedges between which she walked had kindled from the dusty green of summer into long lines of scarlet and yellow flame that danced and flickered against the sagging grey sky in the breeze that flowed through them. All her life she had known that road, and the downs that rose at the end of it, and, beyond them, the wide plains of the sea into which the downs dropped—a sheer fall of eight hundred feet—in scooped precipices of white or rosy chalk.

For she was a native of Netherhinton and had never been further east of it than Bournemouth, further west than Sidcnouth, or further north than Dorchester. She came of poor parents. Her father had been a farm labourer and her mother the daughter of a labourer, and it had been thought a great piece of luck for her to marry the landlord of the Golden Lion.

She walked on at a brisk pace, looking neither to right not left nor even ahead of her: she walked, indeed, not at all as if walking for the mere sake of it, but as one on an errand, and when she reached the end of the road she began at once, without a pause or a glance about her, to climb the down by a sheep track that wavered steeply up it.

Under the stress of the climb her pace became gradually slower and slower; halfway up she paused, breathless, and turned to survey with unseeing eyes the variegated fields below her and, beyond them, the village thatches crouching under the yellowing elms and the gaunt grey fragment of Evesdon Castle, which Cromwell had blown up.

As soon as she had breath enough, she continued her climb, and then, when she was almost at the top and had reached the earthwork, vanished along the long line of the ditch and in half a minute reappeared, clambering on her hands and knees up the steep rampart. Soon she had crawled to the top, and stood for a moment silhouetted against the sky, a minute vertical object breaking the long horizontal lines of down and earthworks. Then again she disappeared.

The grassy area inside the rampart sloped slightly upwards to the sheer edge, so that from where she stood she saw nothing of the sea, but only the grey, laden sky. But she did not want to see the sea, for she knew that today it would be—not as it had been eighteen years ago today, blue and lustrous as an iris-petal and, near the shore, paler and so clear that the ribs of chalky rock at the bottom were as visible as if seen through it flawless, pale blue crystal—but leaden-grey, desolate, chilling to the heart.

So she did not go towards the cliff-edge, but followed the base of the rampart until it bent inwards at right-angles and crossed the hilltop. There she stopped, and in the bend, as if in the corner of a roofless room, sat down. For a while she sat motionless, self-absorbed; then leaned back against the slope of the turf wall, turned on her left side, and closed her eyes.

And soon she knew that he was there, the Jim Ansell of

eighteen years ago. She felt no human touch, no warmth, and his voice had no sound, but he was present to her and she could speak to him, not with her lips, not aloud—for there was no need to speak aloud—but in her heart, with a speech much more real, much more close, than the cold, audible speech she exchanged with her husband and neighbours and the tourists that came to the inn.

And in that unworldly, spiritual speech he answered her. With her eyes and all her senses closed and his visible absence shut out and forgotten, she lay in his arms, felt her body wrapped, safe and sound, in his body, the warmth of his face against hers, the smell, like heather and seaweed, of his khaki jacket. She was alive once more, escaped from the death of her present existence into the warm life of her early days. That life was so real to her that whenever she reached their meeting-place and lay back and closed her eyes, her actual self ceased to exist, and she had never once thought it strange that a tired faded woman of forty should lie in the arms of this dark-haired young man of twenty-two, nor had she ever told herself that their child, if it had lived, would by now have been a boy only five years younger than his father, or that, just as there was another Mary, the faded Mary of today, so there was another Jim Ansell, withered and eyeless, lying in some unknown cemetery in France.

Such thoughts never came to her, for he and she met in a timeless and unchanging world which belonged to them alone. This angle in the earthwork was especially theirs, but they met in other places too, for she carried their secret world within her and could drop back into it whenever opportunity occurred. When she was alone at the inn, working in the kitchen or sitting, darning, in the little private parlour, she would often leave her patient body to get on with its work and would step across the threshold; and at night, the moment the candle had been blown out and she had laid down in bed with Sam, she would be gone, abandoning to her husband the tired, obedient Mary Brakefield like a corpse laid out, hurrying back to her real life and Jim.

But sometimes, when she was very tired, she had not the strength to escape. The outer world—Sam Brakefield, the inn, the neighbours—was too strong for her. She was too feeble, by herself, to support and preserve the world of her desires. If only there had been someone else who knew of it and recognized its reality, who would speak of Jim, who would, perhaps, call her, not Mrs Brakefield, but Mrs Ansell, what a help and what a comfort it would be.

But there was no one: her secret was unshared. That name, Mary Ansell, which she had never borne in real life, was the name by which she thought of herself. She had actually written it in the few books which Jim's mother had left her at her death fourteen years ago. It was safe to do so, for Mary Ansell was the name of Jim's mother, and if Sam had ever noticed it he would not have been surprised.

Mrs Ansell had left her not only the books, but also Jim's scroll, neatly framed—the scroll that had been sent to her after he had been killed. But Sam, as far as Mary knew, had never looked into the books. He had shown no surprise when they and the scroll had been brought to his wife, for he had known that she and Mrs Ansell were old friends. When she had opened the parcel he had lifted up the scroll and examined it. 'It'll look nice on the wall,' he had said, and had then asked: 'Who was he?'

'Her son,' Mary had answered, and she had put away the

books in the hanging bookcase in the parlour and hung up the scroll there. Sam never sat in that room. In the summer, on those days when so many visitors called that there was no more space in the public room, some of them were served there, but for nine months in the year Mary had it to herself, and she would sit there often to sew and darn.

Seated there near the books he must often have read, and with his scroll before her eyes, she felt closer to him than anywhere else but in the earthwork. She often glanced at his name at the bottom of the scroll—Lance-corporal James Ansell—but she seldom read what went before it, for the last sentence—'Let those that come after see to it that his name be not forgotten'—spoke too painfully of his absence, made of him in name only, its name threatened with oblivion.

It was eighteen years ago, eighteen years this very day, that they had met for the last time. On the last day of his leave from France they had climbed the downs together, scrambled up the earthwork, and walked to the edge of the cliff. He had laughed when she had clutched at his sleeve to stop him going too near the brink. The whole immense depth of air below them and the huge expanse of sea sparkled with sunshine. Out near the horizon a ship—an English battleship—drew a long, gauzy trail of smoke after it. Jim pointed to the horizon. 'You'd never think, would you,' he said, 'that thousands of chaps were in the thick of it just over there?'

'Don't,' she said. 'Don't think of it. I don't want to think of it

'Till I'm there?'

She nodded, and they turned away from the cliff and walked across to the angle of the rampart. There they lay down, his arms round her. 'Then you'll *wait* for me?' he whispered half-jokingly. 'Only a few months, till my next leave. Then we'll get married.'

She pressed her cheek against his. 'I don't have to wait,' she said, her heart suddenly full. 'I'm yours already.'

For a while he did not speak. Then he said: 'Yes, you're mine Mary, and I'm Yours. Only we've got to wait till my next leave to be married.'

She shook her head. 'We're married already.'

Again he paused, as if thinking. Then he said: 'But...but suppose I was to stop one?'

'Stop one?'

'Stop a shell or a bullet. Get knocked out.'

She put her hand over his mouth. 'Don't. Don't say such things.'

'But it might happen,' he said, when she had freed his mouth.

'That means we mustn't wait.'

'But think, Mary, what might happen; to you, I mean.'

'I'm thinking,' she said. 'That's wily I say we mustn't wait.'

It was already dark when they walked home together, and parted outside the gate of her home.

A week later, before she had received any letter from him, she was passing his mother's cottage and Mrs Ansell called to her from the door. Mary went to her, and she led her into the little front room, paused to shut the door, then turned on the girl a face woefully transformed. 'Mary,' she said. 'Jim's gone.'

'Gone.' It was as if lightning had struck her. She felt it leap from her head to her heels.

'Killed,' said Mrs Ansell.

When Mary knew she was to have a child she told her mother—weeping, as she spoke, not for shame, but for Jim. Her mother laid her arm round her shoulder. She spoke no word of rebuke, and, though she spoke no word of comfort either, Mary knew that she understood and sympathized. 'I shall have to tell your father,' was all she said.

'Will he be angry?' Mary asked.

'Yes,' said the old woman, 'but I'll manage him. You keep out of his way and say nothing.'

Mary never knew of the encounter between her mother and father, nor that her father had wished to turn her out of doors and had resigned himself only when her mother had told him, that, if Mary went, she would go with her. She knew only that, after that, her father never spoke to her, never took the least notice of her.

Two months later her mother told her that she was to go to an aunt in Devonshire and stay there till after her baby was born. What was to happen after that she did not ask, but she was resolved that, come what might, she would never be separated from the child. But the child, a little boy, was stillborn, and three months after his birth, Mary returned to her home.

It seemed to her that her life was finished. In her absence a new landlord had come to the Golden Lion. He was a bachelor, and her mother now worked at the inn, scrubbing floor and washing-up mugs and glasses. Soon after her return, her mother came home with the news that Mr Brakefield wanted a handy girl to help in the bar and that she had mentioned Mary to him. A few days later Mary began her work at the inn.

At the end of a year, to her amazement and horror, he

asked her to marry him. Ashen-faced and with a trembling lip she refused, but he waved aside her refusal. 'You think it over, my dear,' he said. 'I don't want to hurry you. Think it over and see what your mother says.'

Her mother, when Mary spoke of it, pressed her to accept Brakefield. 'You must think of the future, my dearie,' she said. 'When your father and I are gone you'll have no home. You'll have to toil and moil, perhaps for a hard master or mistress. Mr Brakefield's honest and he's kind. He'll be a good husband to you, Mary. Take him. It'll be a comfort to me to know you're well provided for.'

'But I can't ever forget Jim,' said Mary.

'You don't have to forget him. Keep him to yourself, that's all, and act fairly by your husband.'

'But mustn't I tell him...?'

'About Jim?'

'About the child?'

'No. There's no cause to tell him. No one here knows about it, and never will.'

A month later Mary became Mrs Brakefield.

It was getting dark when Mary Brakefield opened her eyes and found herself alone under the sky in the angle of the rampart. Dazed and chilly, she got to her feet. If she did not hurry she would never find the path down the steep slope. Already when she climbed down the great turf wall and emerged from the ditch, the village below her was lost in the gloom of its elms, and by the time she had reached the foot of the down and struck into the road the last pale streaks in the west were closing into the darkness of a stormy sky.

She felt desolate and tired by her long, lonely ecstasy.

She clung to Jim, trying to keep him with her still, but he withdrew from her. Her spirit was too weak now to hold him, her attention too distracted by the need of keeping her path on the dark road. If only there was someone who knew, someone who would come towards her now, down this dark road, and as he passed her call out: 'Goodnight, Mrs Ansell.' Those few short words would be enough to keep her and Jim together.

But the road was deserted, and, as she turned into the village, large drops of rain began to fall.

When she entered the inn her husband's voice greeted her.

'Two gentlemen wanting tea, Mary. I've got the kettle on and shown them into the parlour, by the fire.'

The two young men had walked all day. They had lunched off beet and bread and cheese at an inn twelve miles away and had hoped to find another inn in the cove they had reached late in the afternoon. But no inn was there, and when they had asked for the nearest they had been directed to Netherhinton, four miles away. Now they sat, tired and contented, in the little parlour of the Golden Lion, one on each side of the fireplace, with their legs stretched to the warmth, waiting for the tea they had ordered.

When he had finished a cigarette, the more energetic of the two got out of his chair and, with his hands in the pockets of his shorts, began prowling round the room, examining the pictures and photographs. When he had reached the bookcase be called to his friend: 'I say, Guy, here's *The Return of the Native*, and *Jude*, and *Lorna Doone*, and the Bible, and *Pickwick*. Not a bad lot for a village inn.'

He took down *Jude the Obscure*, opened the cover, and

read, '*Mary Ansell*, 1919.' *Pickwick* revealed the same name, and then he was interrupted by the opening of the door. A thin-faced woman brought in their tea on a tray. The young man, caught with *Pickwick* in his hand, spoke to her. 'I've found a nice lot of books here,' he said. 'Are they yours?'

The pale, red-rimmed eyes met his. 'Yes, sir,' she said in her tired, toneless voice; 'they're all mine.'

She set the tea on the table. 'Just ring the bell if you want anything, gentlemen,' she said as she went quietly out.

They thanked her, and the other young man rose from his chair and went over to where his friend was standing. 'What's this?' he said, bending his head to inspect Jim's scroll.

'Some poor devil that was killed in the war,' said the first, and he read: '*Lance-corporal James Ansell.*'

'Her son, I expect,' said the other as they sat down to their tea.

When they had finished they rang for the bill, and the thin-faced woman returned. How far was it, they asked, to Wareham?

Six miles, she told them; and there was a bus in twenty minutes' time if they were tired of walking.

'Good! Then, if you don't mind, we'll sit here till it comes.'

'Certainly, sir,' she said, without raising her eyes from the tray on which she was piling the used tea-things.

'Not exactly a cheerful specimen, is she?' said one to the other as they returned to their chairs beside the fire.

Five minutes before the time for the bus they slung their knapsacks on their backs and went out of the room. As they passed the kitchen door it was ajar, and the first young man called out a goodnight as he passed. 'Goodnight, Mrs Ansell,' he called.

She was standing at the kitchen table, her pale eyes cast down, her mouth drooping bitterly at the corners, preparing supper for herself and her husband; but at the sound of the young man's voice her face bloomed suddenly as if kindled by some inner, spiritual light, and her mouth, its bitterness gone, took on the charming, wistful smile of a young girl.

THE LAST LEAF

O. Henry

In a little district west of Washington Square the streets have run crazy and broken themselves into small strips called 'places'. These 'places' make strange angles and curves. One street crosses itself a time or two. An artist once discovered a valuable possibility in this street. Suppose a collector with a bill for paints, paper and canvas should, in traversing this route, suddenly meet himself coming back, without a cent having been paid on account!

So, to quaint old Greenwich Village the art people soon came prowling, hunting for north windows and eighteenth-century gables and Dutch attics and low rents. Then they imported some pewter mugs and a chafing dish or two from Sixth Avenue, and became a 'colony'.

At the top of a squatty, three-storey brick house Sue and Johnsy had their studio. 'Johnsy' was familiar for Joanna. One was from Maine; the other from California. They had met at the *table d'hte* of an Eighth Street 'Delmonico's', and found their tastes in art, chicory salad and bishop sleeves so congenial that the joint studio resulted.

That was in May. In November a cold, unseen stranger,

whom the doctors called Pneumonia, stalked about the colony, touching one here and there with his icy fingers. Over on the east side this ravager strode boldly, smiting his victims by scores, but his feet trod slowly through the maze of the narrow and moss-grown 'places'.

Mr Pneumonia was not what you would call a chivalric old gentleman. A mite of a little woman with blood thinned by California zephyrs was hardly fair game for the red-fisted, short-breathed old duffer. But Johnsy he smote; and she lay, scarcely moving, on her painted iron bedstead, looking through the small Dutch windowpanes at the blank side of the next brick house.

One morning the busy doctor invited Sue into the hallway with a shaggy, grey eyebrow.

'She has one chance in—let us say, ten,' he said, as he shook down the mercury in his clinical thermometer. 'And that chance is for her to want to live. This way people have of lining-up on the side of the undertaker makes the entire pharmacopoeia look silly. Your little lady has made up her mind that she's not going to get well. Has she anything on her mind?'

'She—she wanted to paint the Bay of Naples some day,' said Sue.

'Paint?—bosh! Has she anything on her mind worth thinking twice—a man for instance?'

'A man?' said Sue, with a jew's-harp twang in her voice. 'Is a man worth—but, no, doctor; there is nothing of the kind.'

'Well, it is the weakness, then,' said the doctor. 'I will do all that science, so far as it may filter through my efforts, can accomplish. But whenever my patient begins to count the carriages in her funeral procession I subtract 50 per cent from the curative power of medicines. If you will get her to ask one question about the new winter styles in cloak sleeves I will promise you a one-in-five chance for her, instead of one in ten.'

After the doctor had gone Sue went into the workroom and cried a Japanese napkin to a pulp. Then she swaggered into Johnsy's room with her drawing board, whistling ragtime.

Johnsy lay, scarcely making a ripple under the bedclothes, with her face toward the window. Sue stopped whistling, thinking she was asleep.

She arranged her board and began a pen-and-ink drawing to illustrate a magazine story. Young artists must pave their way to Art by drawing pictures for magazine stories that young authors write to pave their way to literature.

As Sue was sketching a pair of elegant horseshow riding trousers and a monocle of the figure of the hero, an Idaho cowboy, she heard a low sound, several times repeated. She went quickly to the bedside.

Johnsy's eyes were open wide. She was looking out the window and counting—counting backward.

'Twelve,' she said, and little later 'eleven'; and then 'ten,' and 'nine'; and then 'eight' and 'seven', almost together.

Sue look solicitously out of the window. What was there to count? There was only a bare, dreary yard to be seen, and the blank side of the brick house twenty feet away. An old, old ivy vine, gnarled and decayed at the roots, climbed half way up the brick wall. The cold breath of autumn had stricken its leaves from the vine until its skeleton branches clung, almost bare, to the crumbling bricks.

'What is it, dear?' asked Sue.

'Six,' said Johnsy, in almost a whisper. 'They're falling faster now. Three days ago there were almost a hundred. It made my head ache to count them. But now it's easy. There goes another one. There are only five left now.'

'Five what, dear? Tell your Sudie.'

'Leaves. On the ivy vine. When the last one falls I must go, too. I've known that for three days. Didn't the doctor tell you?'

'Oh, I never heard of such nonsense,' complained Sue, with magnificent scorn. 'What have old ivy leaves to do with your getting well? And you used to love that vine so, you naughty girl. Don't be a goosey. Why, the doctor told me this morning that your chances for getting well real soon were—let's see exactly what he said—he said the chances were ten to one! Why, that's almost as good a chance as we have in New York when we ride on the street cars or walk past a new building. Try to take some broth now, and let Sudie go back to her drawing, so she can sell the editor man with it, and buy port wine for her sick child, and pork chops for her greedy self.'

'You needn't get any more wine,' said Johnsy, keeping her eyes fixed out the window. 'There goes another. No, I don't want any broth. That leaves just four. I want to see the last one fall before it gets dark. Then I'll go, too.'

'Johnsy, dear,' said Sue, bending over her, 'will you promise me to keep your eyes closed, and not look out the window until I am done working? I must hand those drawings in by tomorrow. I need the light, or I would draw the shade down.'

'Couldn't you draw in the other room?' asked Johnsy, coldly.

'I'd rather be here by you,' said Sue. 'Beside, I don't want you to keep looking at those silly ivy leaves.'

'Tell me as soon as you have finished,' said Johnsy, closing her eyes, and lying white and still as fallen statue, 'because I want to see the last one fall. I'm tired of waiting. I'm tired of thinking. I want to turn loose my hold on everything, and go sailing down, down, just like one of those poor, tired leaves.'

'Try to sleep,' said Sue. 'I must call Behrman up to be my model for the old hermit miner. I'll not be gone a minute. Don't try to move 'til I come back.'

Old Behrman was a painter who lived on the ground floor beneath them. He was past sixty and had a Michael Angelo's Moses beard curling down from the head of a satyr along with the body of an imp. Behrman was a failure in art. Forty years he had wielded the brush without getting near enough to touch the hem of his Mistress's robe. He had been always about to paint a masterpiece, but had never yet begun it. For several years he had painted nothing except now and then a daub in the line of commerce or advertising. He earned a little by serving as a model to those young artists in the colony who could not pay the price of a professional. He drank gin to excess, and still talked of his coming masterpiece. For the rest he was a fierce little old man, who scoffed terribly at softness in anyone, and who regarded himself as especial mastiff-in-waiting to protect the two young artists in the studio above.

Sue found Behrman smelling strongly of juniper berries in his dimly-lighted den below. In one corner was a blank canvas on an easel that had been waiting there for twenty-five years to receive the first line of the masterpiece. She told him of Johnsy's fancy, and how she feared she would, indeed, light and fragile as a leaf herself, float away, when her slight hold upon the world grew weaker.

Old Behrman, with his red eyes plainly streaming, shouted his contempt and derision for such idiotic imaginings.

'Vass!' he cried. 'Is dere people in de world mit der

foolishness to die because leafs dey drop off from a confounded vine? I haf not heard of such a thing. No, I will not bose as a model for your fool hermit-dunderhead. Vy do you allow dot silly pusiness to come in der brain of her? Ach, dot poor leetle Miss Yohnsy.'

'She is very ill and weak,' said Sue, 'and the fever has left her mind morbid and full of strange fancies. Very well, Mr Behrman, if you do not care to pose for me, you needn't. But I think you are a horrid old—old flibbertigibbet.'

'You are just like a woman!' yelled Behrman. 'Who said I will not bose? Go on. I come mit you. For half an hour I haf peen trying to say dot I am ready to bose. Gott! dis is not any blace in which one so goot as Miss Yohnsy shall lie sick. Some day I vill baint a masterpiece, and ve shall all go away. Gott! yes.'

Johnsy was sleeping when they went upstairs. Sue pulled the shade down to the window-sill, and motioned Behrman into the other room. In there they peered out the window fearfully at the ivy vine. Then they looked at each other for a moment without speaking. A persistent, cold rain was falling, mingled with snow. Behrman, in his old blue shirt, took his seat as the hermit miner on an upturned kettle for a rock.

When Sue awoke from an hour's sleep the next morning she found Johnsy with dull, wide-open eyes staring at the drawn green shade.

'Pull it up; I want to see,' she ordered, in a whisper.

Wearily Sue obeyed.

But, lo! after the beating rain and fierce gusts of wind that had endured through the livelong night, there yet stood out against the brick wall one ivy leaf. It was the last one on the vine. Still dark green near its stem, with its serrated edges tinted with the yellow of dissolution and decay, it hung bravely from the branch some twenty feet above the ground.

'It is the last one,' said Johnsy. 'I thought it would surely fall during the night. I heard the wind. It will fall today, and I shall die at the same time.'

'Dear, dear!' said Sue, leaning her worn face down to the pillow, 'think of me, if you won't think of yourself. What would I do?'

But Johnsy did not answer. The lonesomest thing in all the world is a soul when it is making ready to go on its mysterious, far journey. The fancy seemed to possess her more strongly as one by one the ties that bound her to friendship and to earth were loosed.

The day wore away, and even through the twilight they could see the lone ivy leaf clinging to its stem against the wall. And then, with the coming of the night the north wind was again loosed, while the rain still beat against the windows and pattered down from the low Dutch eaves.

When it was light enough Johnsy, the merciless, commanded that the shade be raised.

The ivy leaf was still there.

Johnsy lay for a long time looking at it. And then she called to Sue, who was stirring her chicken broth over the gas stove.

'I've been a bad girl, Sudie,' said Johnsy. 'Something has made that last leaf stay there to show me how wicked I was. It is a sin to want to die. You may bring me a little broth now, and some milk with a little port in it, and—no; bring me a hand-mirror first, and then pack some pillows about me, and I will sit up and watch you cook.'

And hour later she said:

'Sudie, some day I hope to paint the Bay of Naples.'

The doctor came in the afternoon, and Sue had an excuse to go into the hallway as he left.

'Even chances,' said the doctor, taking Sue's thin, shaking hand in his. 'With good nursing you'll win. And now I must see another case I have downstairs. Behrman, his name is—some kind of an artist, I believe. Pneumonia, too. He is an old, weak man, and the attack is acute. There is no hope for him; but he goes to the hospital today to be made more comfortable.'

The next day the doctor said to Sue: 'She's out of danger. You won. Nutrition and care now—that's all.'

And that afternoon Sue came to the bed where Johnsy lay, contentedly knitting a very blue and very useless woollen shoulder scarf, and put one arm around her, pillows and all.

'I have something to tell you, white mouse,' she said. 'Mr Behrman died of pneumonia today in the hospital. He was ill only two days. The janitor found him the morning of the first day in his room downstairs helpless with pain. His shoes and clothing were wet through and icy cold. They couldn't imagine where he had been on such a dreadful night. And then they found a lantern, still lighted, and a ladder that had been dragged from its place, and some scattered brushes, and a palette with green and yellow colours mixed on it, and—look out the window, dear, at the last ivy leaf on the wall. Didn't you wonder why it never fluttered or moved when the wind blew? Ah, darling, it's Behrman's masterpiece—he painted it there the night that the last leaf fell.'

THE DUENNA

Marie Belloc Lowndes

I

Laura Delacourt, after a long and gallant defence of what those who formed the old-fashioned world to which she belonged would have called her virtue, had capitulated to the entreaties of Julian Trevilic. They had been friends—from tomorrow they would be lovers.

As she lay enfolded in his arms, her head resting on his breast, while now and again their lips met in a trembling clinging kiss, the strangest and, in some ways, the most incongruous thoughts flitted shadow-wise through her mind, mingled with terror at the possible though not the probably, consequence of her surrender.

Her husband, Roger Delacourt, was thirty years older than herself. Though still a vigorous man, he had come to a time of life when even a vigorous man longs instinctively for warmth; so he had left London the day after Christmas Day to join a friend's yacht for a month's cruise in the Mediterranean. And now, just a week later, the wife who he considered a negligible quantity in his self-indulgent, still agreeable existence, had consented to embark on what she knew must be a perilous adventure in a one-storeyed stone house, well named The Folly, built by Julian Treville's great-grandfather.

Long, low, fantastic—it stood at the narrow end of a wide lake on the confines of his property; and a French dancer, known in the Paris of her day as *La Belle Julie*, had spent there a lifetime in exile.

Though Laura in her lover's arms felt strangely at peace, her homing joy was threaded with terror. Constantly her thoughts reverted to her child, David, who, till the man who now held her so closely to him had come into her life, had been the only thing that made that then mournful life worth living.

The boy was spending the New Year with his mother's one close woman friend and her houseful of happy children, so Laura hoped her little son did not miss her. At any other time the thought that this might be so would have stabbed her with unreasonable pain, but what now filled her heart with shrinking fear was the dread thought of David's father, and of the punishment he would exact if he found her out.

Like so many men of his type and generation Roger Delacourt had a poor opinion of women. He believed that the woman tempted always falls. But, again true to type, he made, in this one matter, an exception as to his own wife. That Laura might be tempted was a possibility which never entered his shrewd and cynical mind; and had he been compelled to admit the temptation, he would have felt confident as to her power of resistance. So it was that she faced the awful certainty that were she ever 'found out,' immediate separation from her son, followed by a divorce, would be her punishment.

She had been a child of seventeen when her mother

had elected to sell her into the slavery of marriage with the voluptuary to whom she had now been married ten years. For three years she had been her husband's plaything, and then, suddenly, when their boy was about two years old, he had tired of her. Even so, they lived, both in London and in the country, under the same roof, and many of the people about them thought the Delacourts got on better than do most modern couples. They were, however, often apart for weeks at a time, for Roger Delacourt still hunted, still shot, still fished, with unabated zest, and his wife did none of these things.

As time went on, Laura's joyless life was at once illumined and shadowed by her passionate love for her child, for all great love brings with it fear. A year ago, by his father's decree, David had been sent to a noted preparatory school, leaving his young mother forlornly lonely. It was then that she had met Julian Treville.

By one of those odd accidents of which human life is full, he and she had been the only two guests of an aged brother and sister, distant connections of Laura's own, in a Yorkshire country house. Cousin John and Cousin Mary had watched the sudden friendship with approval. 'Dear Laura Delacourt is just the friend for Julian Treville,' said old Mary to old John. She had added, pensively, 'It is so very nice for a nice young man to have a nice married woman as a nice friend.'

That had been eight months ago, and since then Treville had altered the whole of his life for Laura's sake, she, till today, taking everything and giving nothing, as is so often the way with a woman who believes herself to be good...

During their long drive the lovers scarcely spoke; to be alone together, as they were now, was sufficient bliss.

Treville had met her at a distant railway junction where a motor had been hired in the name of 'Mrs Darcy.' This was part of the plan which was to make the few who must perforce know of her presence at The Folly believe her there as the guest of Treville's stepmother, who was now abroad.

Darcy had been Laura's maiden name, and it was the only name she felt she had the right to call herself. She and her lover were both amateurs in the most dangerous and most exciting drama for which a man and woman can be cast.

The hireling motor had brought them across wide stretches of solitary downland, but now they were speeding through one of the long avenues of Treville Place, their journey nearly at an end.

His neighbours would have told you that Julian Treville was a reserved, queer kind of chap. Laura Delacourt was the first woman he had ever loved; and even now, in this hour or unexpected, craved-for joy, he was asking himself if even his great love gave him the right to make her run what seemed an exceedingly slight risk of detection and consequent disgrace.

Each felt a sense of foreboding, though Laura's reason told her that her terrors were vain, and that it was conscience alone that made her feel afraid. Every possible danger had been countered by her companion. Her pride, her delicacy, her sense of shame—was it false shame?—had been studied by him with a selfless devotion which had deeply moved her. Thus he was leaving her to spend a lonely evening, tended by the old Frenchwoman, who, together with her husband, waited on The Folly's infrequent occupants.

The now aged couple in their hot youth had been on the losing side in the Paris Commune of 1871. They had been saved from imprisonment, possibly worse, by Julian Treville's grandmother, a lawless, high-minded Scotchwoman who called herself a Liberal. She had brought them to England, and for fifty odd years they had lived in a cottage a quarter of a mile from The Folly. There was small reason, as Treville could have argued with perfect truth, to be afraid of this old pair. But Laura did feel afraid, and so it had been arranged between the lovers that only tomorrow, after she had spent at The Folly a solitary night and day, would he, at the close of a day's hunting, share 'Mrs Darcy's' simple dinner...

The motor stopped, and the man and woman, who had been clasped in each other's arms, drew quickly apart.

'We have to get out here,' muttered Treville, 'for there is no carriage-way down to The Folly. I'll carry your bag.'

Keeping up the sorry comedy she paid off and dismissed the chauffeur.

In the now fading daylight Laura saw that to her left the ground sloped steeply down to the shores of a lake whose now grey waters narrowed to a point beyond which there stood a low, pillared building. It was more like an eighteenth-century orangery than a house meant for human habitation. Eerily beautiful, and yet exceedingly desolate, to Laura The Folly appeared unreal—a fairy dwelling in that Kingdom of Romance whither her feet had never strayed, rather than a place where men and women had joyed and sorrowed, lived and died.

'If only I could feel that you will never regret that you came here,' Treville whispered.

She answered quickly, 'I shall always be glad, not sorry, Julian.'

He took her hand and raised it to his lips. Then he said: 'Old Célestine will have it that The Folly is haunted *by La*

Belle Julie. You're not afraid of ghosts, my dearest?'

Laura smiled a little wanly in the twilight. 'Far more afraid of flesh and blood than ghosts,' she murmured. 'Where do Célestine and her husband live, Julian?'

'We can't see their cottage from here; but it's quite close by.' His voice sank: 'I've told them that you're not afraid of being in the house alone at night.'

They went down a winding footpath, she clinging to him for the very joy in his nearness, till they reached the stone-paved space which lay between the shore of the lake and the low grey building. And then, suddenly, while they were walking towards the high front door, Laura gave a stifled cry, for a gnome-like figure had sprung, as if from nowhere, across their path.

'Here's old Jacques,' exclaimed Treville vexedly. 'He always shows an excess of zeal!'

The little Frenchman was gesticulating and talking eagerly, explaining that fires had been burning all day in the three rooms which were to be occupied by the visitor. He further told, at unnerving length, that Célestine would be at The Folly herself very shortly to install 'Madame'.

When the old chap had shuffled off, Julian Treville put a key in the lock of the heavy old door; taking Laura's slight figure up into his strong arms, he lifted her over the threshold straight into an enchanting living-room where nothing had been altered for over a hundred years.

She gave a cry of delight. 'What a delicious place, Julian! I never thought it would be like this—'

A long fire threw up high flames in the deep fireplace, and a lighted lamp stood on a round, gilt-rimmed, marble table close to a low and roomy, if rather stiff, square armchair. The few pieces of fine Empire furniture were covered with faded yellow satin which had been brought from Paris when Napoleon was ironing out the frontiers of Europe, for the Treville of that day had furnished The Folly to please the Frenchwoman he loved. The walls of the room were hung with turquoise silk. There was a carved-wood gilt mirror over the mantelpiece, and on the right-hand wall there hung an oval pastel of *La Belle Julie.*

Hand in hand they stood, looking up at the lovely smiling face.

'According to tradition,' said Treville, 'that picture was the only thing the poor soul brought with her when she left France. The powdered hair proves it must have been done when Julie was in her teens, before the Revolution. My great-great-grandfather fell in love with her when she must have been well over thirty—'

Then, dropping the mask he had worn since they had left the motor, 'Laura!' he exclaimed; 'Beloved! At last-at last!'

For him, and for her, too, the world sank away, though, even so that which is now called her subconscious self was listening, full of shrinking fear, for the sound of a key in the lock...

He said at last in a low, shaken voice, 'And now I suppose that I must leave you?'

Her lips formed the words telling him that he had been overscrupulous in his care for her, that they might as well brave the curious eyes of old Célestine tonight as tomorrow. And then, before she could utter them, there came the sound of steps on the stone path outside.

'It's Célestine, come before her time,' muttered Treville.

The front door opened and Laura, turning round quickly,

saw a tall, thin, old woman, clad in a black stuff dress; a white Muslin cap lay on her white hair, and over her shoulders a fur cape.

Standing just within the door, which she had shut behind her, she cast a long, measuring glance at her master, and at the lady who had come to spend a week at The Folly at this untoward time of the year.

It was a kindly, even an indulgent, glance, but it made Laura feel suddenly afraid.

'I come to ask,' exclaimed Célestine in very fair English, 'if Madame is comfortable? Is there anything I can do for Madame besides laying the table and cooking Madame's dinner?'

'I don't think so—everything is delightful,' murmured Laura.

The old woman, taking a few steps forward, vanished into what the newcomer was soon to learn was the dining-room.

Treville said wistfully, 'And now I must leave you.'

Laura whispered faintly, 'I am a coward, Julian.'

He answered eagerly, 'I would not have you other than what you are.'

She took his hand in hers, and laid it against her cheek.

'It's because of David—only because of David—that I feel afraid.'

And as she said the word 'afraid,' the old Frenchwoman came back into the room. 'Would Madame like me to come in to sleep each night?' she asked.

Treville answered for Laura. 'Mrs Darcy prefers being here alone. She will live as does my stepmother, when she is staying at The Folly.'

He turned to Laura. 'I will say goodnight now, but after

I come in from hunting tomorrow I'll come down, as you have kindly asked me to do, to dinner.'

She answered in a low voice, 'I shall be so glad to see you tomorrow evening.'

'By the way—' he waited a moment.

Why did Célestine stand there, looking at them? Why didn't she go away, as she would have hastened to do if his companion had been his stepmother?

But at last he ended his sentence with '—there's a private telephone from The Folly to my study, if you have occasion to speak to me.'

After her lover had left her with a quiet clasp of the hand, and after old Célestine had gone off, at last, to her own quarters, Laura sat down and covered her face with her hands; she felt both happy and miserable, exultant and afraid.

At last, she threw a tender thought to *La Belle Julie*, who had given up everything that to her should have seemed worth living for, in a material sense, to follow the man she loved into what must have been a piteous exile. And yet Laura felt tonight that she too would have had that cruel courage, had she not been the mother of a child.

She got up at last, and walked across the room, wondering how lovely Julie had fared during the long, weary hours she must have waited here for her lover.

Would the Treville of that day have done for his Julie what Julian had done for his Laura tonight? Would he have respected her cowardly fears? She felt sure not. Julie's Treville might have gone away, but Julie's Treville would have come back. Well, she knew that Laura's Treville would not return tonight.

And then she turned round quickly, for across the still

air of the room had fallen the sound of a deep sigh.

Swiftly, Laura went across to the door, masked by a stiff curtain of tapestry, which led into the corridor linking the various rooms of The Folly.

She lifted the curtain, and slipped out into the dimly lit corridor, but there was no one there.

Coming back into the sitting-room she sat down again by the fire, convinced that her nerves had played her a trick, and once more she found herself thinking *of La Belle Julie.* She felt as if there was a bond between herself and the long dead dancer; the bond which links all poor women who embark on the danger-fraught adventure of secret, illicit love.

II

That evening Célestine proved that her hand had not lost its French cunning. But Laura was too excited, as well as too tired, to eat. The old woman made no comment as to that, but when at last she found with delight that 'Mrs Darcy' spoke excellent French, she did tell her that if she heard strange sighs, or maybe a stifled sob, she was not to feel afraid, as it would only be the wraith *of La Belle Julie* expatiating her sin where that sin had not only been committed but exulted in.

But it was not the ghost of Julie of whom Laura was afraid—it was Célestine, with her gleaming brown eyes and shrewd face, whom she feared. She breathed more easily when the old Frenchwoman was gone...

The bedchamber where she was to sleep had also been left unaltered for a hundred years and more. It was hung with faded lavender silk, and on the floor lay an Aubusson carpet, while at the farther end of the room was the wide, low, *Directoire* bed which had been brought from the Paris of the young Napoleon.

The telephone of which Treville had told her stood on a table close to her pillow. How amazed would Julie have been to hear that a day would come when a woman lying in what had been her bed would be able to speak from there to her lover—the man who, like Julie's own lover, was master of the great house which stood over a mile away from The Folly.

Célestine had forgotten to draw the heavy embroidered yellow silk curtains, and Laura walked to the nearest window and looked out on to the gleaming waters of the lake.

Across to the right rose dense clumps of dark ilexes; to the left tall trees, now stripped of leaves, stood black and dreary against the winter sky.

The telephone bell tinkled. She turned and ran across the room, and then she heard Julian Treville's voice as strong, as clear, as love-laden, as if he were with her here, tonight.

The next day's sun illumined a beautiful soft winter morning, and Laura felt not only tremblingly happy, but also what she had not thought to feel—at peace. She went for a walk round the lake, then enjoyed the luncheon Célestine had prepared for her. Célestine, so much was clear, was set on waiting on her far more assiduously than she did on her own mistress, old Mrs Treville.

About three o'clock Laura went again out of doors, to come in, an hour later, to find the lamp in the drawing-room lit, though it was not yet dark.

She went through into her bedroom, and then she heard the telephone ring—not loudly, insistently, as it had rung last night, but with a thin, tenuous sound.

Eagerly she went over to the side of the bed and took off the receiver, and then, as if coming from infinitely far away, she heard Julian Treville's voice.

'Are you there, my darling? I am in darkness, but our love is my beacon, and my heart is full of you,' and his voice, his dear voice, sank away...

Then he was home from hunting far sooner than he had thought to be? This surely meant that very soon he would be here.

She took off her hat and coat put on a frock Julian had once said he loved to see her wear, and then went back to wait for his coming in the sitting-room. But the moments became minutes, and the minutes quarters of an hour, and the time went by very slowly.

At last a key turned in the lock of the front door, and she stood up—then felt a pang of bitter disappointment, for it was only the old Frenchwoman who passed through into the room.

Célestine shut the door behind her, and then she came close up to where Laura had sat down again, wearily, by the fire.

'Madame!' she exclaimed. And then she stopped short, a tragic look on her pale withered face.

Laura's thoughts flew to her child. She leapt up from her chair. 'What is it, Célestine? A message for me?'

Very solemnly Célestine said the fearful words: 'Prepare for ill news.'

'Ill news?' Oh! how could she have left her child? 'What do you mean?' cried Laura violently.

'There is no message come for you. But—but—our good kind master, Mr Treville, is dead. He was killed out hunting today. I was in the village when the news was brought.' She went on speaking in quick gasps: 'His horse—how say you?—' she waited, and then, finding the word she sought, 'stumbled,' she sobbed.

Laura for a moment stood still, as if she had not heard, or did not understand the purport of the other's words, and then she gave a strangled cry, as Célestine, gathering her to her gaunt breast, said quickly in French, 'My poor, poor lady! Well did I see that my master loved you—and that you loved him. You must leave The Folly tonight, at once. They have already telegraphed for old Mrs Treville.'

III

An hour later Laura was dressed, ready for departure. In a few minutes from now Célestine would be here to carry her bag to the car which the old Frenchwoman had procured to take her to the distant station where Julian Tireville had met her yesterday? It seemed aeons of time ago.

Suddenly there came a loud knock on the heavy door, and at once she walked across the room and opened it wide.

Nothing mattered to her now; and when Roger Delacourt strode into the room she felt scarcely any surprise, and that though she had believed him a thousand miles away.

'Are you alone, Laura?' he asked harshly.

There was a look of savage anger in his face. His vanity—the vanity of a man no longer young who has had a strong allure for women—felt bruised in its tenderest part.

As she said nothing, only looking at him with an air of tragic pain and defiance, he went on, jeeringly, 'No doubt you are asking yourself how I found out where you were, and on what pretty business you were engaged? I will give you a clue, and you can guess the rest for yourself. I had to come back unexpectedly to England, and the one person to whom you gave this address—I presume so you might have news of the boy—unwittingly gave you away!'

She still said nothing, and he went on bitterly: 'I thought you—fool that I was—a good woman. But from what I hear I now know that your lover, Julian Treville, is no new friend. But I do not care, I do enquire, how often you have been here—'

'This is the first time,' she said dully, 'that I have been here.'

And then it was as if something outside herself impelled her to add the untrue words, 'I am not, as you seem to think, Roger, alone—' for with a sharp thrill of intense fear she had remembered her child.

'Not alone?' he repeated incredulously. And then he saw the tapestried curtain which hung over the door, opposite to where he stood, move, and he realized that someone was behind it, listening.

He took a few steps forward, and pulled the curtain roughly back. But the dimly illumined corridor was empty; whoever had been there eavesdropping had scurried away into shelter.

He came back to the spot where he had been standing before. Baffled, angry, still full of doubt, and yet, deep in his heart, unutterably relieved. Already, a half-suspicion that Laura was sheltering some woman friend engaged in an intrigue had flashed into his mind, and the suspicion crystallized into certainty as he looked loweringly into her pale, set face. She did not look as more than once, in the days of his good fortunes, he had seen a guilty wife look.

Yes, that must be the solution of this queer secret escapade! Laura, poor fool! had been the screen behind which hid a pair of guilty lovers. Thirty years ago a woman had played the same thankless part in an intrigue of his own.

'Who is your friend?' he asked roughly.

Her lips did not move, and he told himself, with a certain satisfaction, that she was paralysed with fear.

'How long have you and your friend been here? That, at least, you can tell me.'

At last she whispered what sounded like the absurd answer, 'Just a hundred years.'

Then, turning quickly, she went through the door which gave into the dining-room, and shut it behind her.

Roger Delacourt began pacing about the room; he felt what he had very seldom come to feel in his long, hard, if till now fortunate, life, just a little foolish, but relieved—unutterably relieved—and glad.

The Folly? Well named indeed! The very setting for a secret love-affair. Beautiful, too, in its strange and romantic aloofness from everyday life.

He went and gazed up at the pastel, which was the only picture in the room. What an exquisite, flower-like face! It reminded him of a French girl he had known when he was a very young man. Her name had been Zelie Mignard, and she had been reader-companion to an old marquise with whose son he had spent a long summer and autumn on the Loire. From the first moment he had seen Zelie she had attracted him violently, and though little more than a boy, he had made up his mind to seduce her. But she had resisted him, and then, in spite of himself, he had come to love her with that ardent first love which returns no more.

Suddenly there fell on the air of the still room the sound of a long, deep sigh. He wheeled sharply round to see that between himself and the still uncurtained window there stood a slender young woman—Laura's peccant friend, without a doubt!

He could not see her very clearly, yet of that he was not sorry, for he was not and he had never been—he told himself with an inward chuckle—the man to spoil sport.

Secretly he could afford to smile at the thought of his cold, passionless wife acting as duenna. Hard man as he was, his old heart warmed to the erring stranger, the more so that her sudden apparition had removed a last lingering doubt from his mind.

She threw out her slender hands with a gesture that again seemed to fill his mind with memories of his vanished youth, and there floated across the dark room the whispered words 'Be not unkind.' And then—did she say, 'Remember Zelie?'

No, no—it was his heart, less atrophied than he had thought it to be, which had evoked, quickened into life, the name of his first love, the French girl who, if alive, must be—hateful, disturbing thought—an old woman today.

Then, as he gazed at her, the shadowy figure swiftly walked across the room, and so through the tapestry curtain.

He waited a moment, then slowly passed through the dining-room, and so into the firelit bedroom beyond.

His wife was standing by the window, looking as wraith-like as had done, just now, her friend. She was staring out into the darkness, her arms hanging by her side. She had not turned round when she had heard the door of the room open.

'Laura!' said her husband gruffly. And then she turned and cast on him a suffering alien glance.

'I accept your explanation of your presence here. And, well, I apologise for my foolish suspicions. Still you're not a child! The part you're playing is not one any man would wish his wife to play. How long do you—and your friend—intend to stay here?'

'We meant to stay ten days,' she said listlessly, 'but as you're home, Roger, I'll leave now, if you like.'

'And your friend, Laura, what of her?'

'I think she has already left The Folly.'

She waited a moment, then forced herself to add, 'Julian Treville was killed today out hunting—as I suppose you know.'

'Good God! How awful! Believe me, I did not know—'

Roger Delacourt was sincerely affected, as well he might be, for already he had arranged, in his own mind, to go to Leicestershire next week.

And, strange to say, as the two travelled up to town together, he was more considerate in his manner to his wife than he had been for many years. For one thing, he felt that this curious episode proved Laura to have more heart than he had given her credit for. But, being the manner of man and of husband he happened to be, he naturally did not approve of her having risked her spotless reputation in playing the part of duenna to a friend who had loved not wisely but too well. He trusted that what had just happened would prove a lesson to his wife and, for the matter of that, to himself.

THE PILLAR OF HELIODOROS

Anonymous

> *The only Yavana (Greek) king whose name has yet been found on an Indian monument is Antialcidas. At Besnagar, near Bhilra in the former Gwalior State is a stone column once crowned by a figure of Garuda. The inscription records that it was erected in honour of Krishna (Vasueleva) by a Greek named Heliodoros, son of Dion, who had come to Vidisa as an ambassador from Antialcidas, King of Taxila to King Kasiputra Bhagabhadra. The inscription is full of interest as proving that a Greek had adopted an Indian faith and as evidencing the contact which was then (2nd century BC) taking place between Malwa and the Greek kingdoms.*

Taxila's great city wall stood boldly against the clear shining green sky of an early spring day in the year 140 BC. It was sunset and the doves, bulbuls, parakeets and crows were homing to their nests in hundreds. Outside the western gate a small group of men were watching the road. A thick cloud of dust clearly marked the route. Apparently, a cavalcade was approaching. As it drew near, the watchers could distinguish a band of horsemen escorting an elephant on which sat a young lad, evidently a person of some importance. When the portal was reached the mahout touched the beast and rearing its trunk it saluted with loud trumpetings. Then with heavings to and fro it knelt and the boy descended. Immediately, an elderly man stepped forward from the waiting group. His countenance was grave yet kindly, dignified with refined features, and the respect shown to him by his companions indicated a position of authority. He was, in fact, Dion the royal chamberlain.

His voice was kindly as he greeted the young stranger. 'Welcome, Prince Bhadrasena to our land. My master, great Antialcidas, has ordered me to see to thy comfort for tonight. Tomorrow, when thou hast rested he would talk with thee. This is my only son, Heliodoros, even now a student at the university,' and turning, he presented a young man to the prince.

The company entered the city and mounting some gaily caparisoned horses were soon riding down the broad high street. Taxila was a town of great importance, the first large Indian city at which merchants who had come down the Kabul valley and crossed the Indus above Attock arrived. The streets were filled with a jostling crowd. Sturdy, vigorous men of the Hindu Kush, who had brought their highland-bred horses to sell in this city outside which stretched the wide, open plain where many a gay hawking party rode, rubbed shoulders with students from all corners of Hindustan. Taxila was famous as a centre of learning and to it scholars of all classes flocked for instruction.

As the little company passed along, Dion pointed out the various buildings of interest. Near the gate by which they had entered stood the king's palace. A poor place for a sovereign, thought Bhadrasena. True, it was large, but of sombre grey stone and with little decoration it looked to him just the same as the buildings on either side of the wide street. Their flat roofs were of mud; only narrow, slit windows looked on to the street, most of the rooms facing inwards, towards the courtyard.

This was really the university quarters, Heliodoros explained. Here the prince would reside. The chamberlain's house was farther down the street, near the great Buddhist temple. And there they dismounted.

The next morning Bhadra rose early. This strange, strong land interested him. His father, King of Vidisa, had sent him to study the Vedas but the lad felt that there were other things worth studying in this northern outpost of India. He dressed himself with care for the interview with King Antialcidas, then stepped to the verandah which faced northwards. What a wall of magic encircling the beautiful river valley was this white wonder of snow-capped hills!

Antialcidas received the prince with ceremonious kindness. A fine, upstanding man was this keeper of the country through which passed the great trade route from the ford at Und to the fertile south. His complexion was of the colour of ripe wheat. Full cheeks, straight nose and firm chin showed his descent from the Greeks. He alone wore a round, flat cap of vividly embroidered cloth.

For many months the fear of a northern invasion had hung over the king's council. It was imperative to strengthen the army and what better unit than a strong elephant corps? These beasts were found at their best in Malwa and the father of this boy ruled in Vidisa, part of that land. It was wise to make friends with such a one.

Bhadrasena bent to the ground as he presented his father's

gifts to Taxila. The noblest was the huge animal, Moti, which he had ridden yesterday when he came to the town. She was outside in the palace courtyard, dressed in all the ornaments and housings for parade on occasions of state. A frontlet of gold and silver diaper with fringes of fish-shaped ornaments in thin beaten silver, necklaces of large silver hawkbells and hanging chains of silver cartouches decked her. Above towered the howdah glittering with gilded plates; all shone resplendently as the sun's rays beat down. The interview over, Dion charged Heliodoros to show their guest the city's sights.

'Hast seen a tiger, a mighty little cat?' he queried.

'Many,' was the astounding reply. 'With my gracious father I often hunted the striped one.'

The grey-blue eyes of the northerner widened. One of Taxila's great sights was the royal menagerie of wild beasts. Outside the northern gate deep pits had been dug and here behind strong bars the leopard, the tiger and even the lion paced the weary paths of captivity. But it would be no pleasure to show these beasts to a boy who knew them in their own haunts. Perhaps this dark-eyed, rather silent youth cared for old places. There were many such around.

'Wouldst see a fire-sanctuary?' Bhadra nodded and they proceeded toward the outskirts of the town. Suddenly the Hindu pulled the sleeve of the other's coat.

'What are these; what does this mean; why are these men chaffering?'

'Oh, this is the square where dowerless maids are sold. No men will marry them. What luck to pass on a market day!'

'Luck!' The stranger shuddered. He could not openly condemn a practice of his hosts but he need not stand and watch. 'Let's go,' he said.

To Heliodoros so common a sight needed no remark and they wandered on through the flowering mustard fields, a lovely yellow scented carpet spread in all directions, till they reached the fire-temple. Taxila was a cosmopolitan city. Its faiths were cosmopolitan too. Buddhists, Jains, Brahmins and Fire worshippers dwelt together in amity. Dion was a Greek and faithful to his father's gods but to his son, reared in an atmosphere of religious tolerance, all gods were much alike.

In the fire-temple's priest he had a friend who allowed him at the close of day to climb the steps leading to the summit where in an ecstasy of delight Heliodoros watched the planets in their courses. Bhadrasena also loved the stars; he had visited Ujjain where astronomy and astrology were the chief studies of the pundits and so to him this shrine with its white shining walls and brazen tablets telling of the deeds of Porus and of Alexander were interesting enough.

As they turned homewards his heart gave a great leap. In the white dust of the roadside were some ascetics. How many had he seen in Vidisa! Naked, ash-coloured and motionless they sat. The cold biting winds sweeping across the plain in winter, the rays of summer sun so intense that bare feet scorched when they touched the stones were to them as nothing. Both youths made obeisance as they passed; such holiness all men held in reverence.

That evening when the sky was rose-red Bhadra said 'Goodbye' to his attendants. Only one remained with the prince who felt that he could never be happy in this dour land. To his eyes accustomed to the giant trees of Central India those around Taxila were stunted. Nowhere could he see the mango-twig so pink, so green unfolding; nowhere did the *palas* tree suddenly cover its black, snake-like branches with rich red blossoms, nowhere did the mischievous, chattering monkey charm the lonely hours. Alas! how true it was that only by painful discipline was wisdom attained.

Spring, lovely dainty spring passed rapidly but before the hot summer winds blew over the fields the young man and boy were friends. Heliodoros had entered manhood for he was twenty-two years old, but he still had much of the young spirit of Greece in his composition, whereas the mind of Bhadrasena was older than his fifteen years. The two found delight in each other's company. The scanty rains broke in July and brought some relief from the pitiless heat. To slip out of the dark house at dawn, to run across the fields to where the deep river flowed, then to strip and plunge under the cool water was sheer delight. One day, however, the Hindu woke shivering and when his friend called him he could not rise. Dion's family was devoted to the sick boy. Their own physician, the senior professor of the medical college, attended him and when the fever broke Dion's wife carried him to her own house and nursed him back to health. It was now that the souls of gay Heliodoros and of quiet Bhadra became as one. The latter was playing one morning with some crested bulbuls when his friend, greatly excited, entered the room.

'Guess, where I am going,' he called.

'To Greece.'

'No, try again.'

'I can't, my head is all muzzy.'

'Well, to your father's court.'

'What! am I returning. Do you go with me?'

'No, my lad. I, yes I, go as ambassador,' and he made a ludicrously solemn salute.

Tears filled the younger's eyes. What bliss to go to Vidisa!

Why was it denied to him? But he conquered his bitter disappointment and replied 'That's good. My father, King Bhagabhadra will be honoured to have such a great ambassador at his court. But when and why?'

'When? As soon as my things are ready. Why? I carry instructions in a letter for his majesty.'

'Lucky you! Well, I must get some presents and write a letter for you to take to my home.'

A few weeks later another group of horsemen had gathered at the western gate; this time to speed the departing traveller. Dion wished to ride with his son as far as the narrow pass through which the road to Hindustan ran. There they halted, the father sad at heart as he looked on the weird, dun-coloured ravine country. A bad beginning for a journey into an unknown land, it seemed to him. Would the lad return safely? Alas! only the gods knew, for on their laps lay the future.

Heliodoros set out with his few soldier companions, faring on, day and night through forests, over deserts, across swamps and rivers. One evening, the muddy, swollen waters of the Lutudri (Sutlej) forced them to halt on its banks. A winter storm had broken the day before and it was impossible to ford the river. Whilst preparations were being made for the night's camp the young leader wandered alone. The way was obscure and he almost stumbled over a huddled object which he saw, as it slowly and with many grunts unfolded itself, to be an old, old man.

'Art thou hurt father?' he enquired.

'Nay, my son,' was the mumbled reply as the old man painfully stood up. At last he was erect but sank to the ground again, exclaiming 'Yavana! Yavana!' Heliodoros helped him to rise once more, saying 'Why Yavana, father? Come, rest and tell me thy story,' and he led the way to the camp. The flickering fire-light showed that the way-farer had passed the usual limits of man's life. Toothless, bleared and feeble he was as one left behind by time. The men made him comfortable on a pile of saddle-bags and gave him a strong, hot drink. As the warmth crept through his withered limbs he seemed rejuvenated and looking at the Greek said clearly, 'Yes, Yavanas came and the horse was grey.'

'What horse? Where was it? Tell us.'

'I forget. I was only up to my father's knee when I saw it. We were on the banks of a great stream. Maybe it was this. Maybe not. I remember I had caught a fish when out of the forest beyond, came a great horse, grey like a rain-cloud. A mighty army came after. Loud drums beat and I was feared so that we hid behind a bush. But I forget,' and the shaking head drooped.

'Some more wine,' whispered the eager listener.

So the strong wine was given and the thin, piping voice went on. 'My father said it was the king's horse and no one must stop it. Then another army came, tall men, riding like gods, and one who rode near where we lay looked like thee. My father said he was a Yavana. The two armies fought. Oh, such blood and noise! I hid my face and when I looked up the horse was wandering away.'

Heliodoros gazed at the speaker. He must have seen the sacred horse as it ranged from field to field followed by an army which, if unconquered after a year, gave to the one who had sent it forth the right to call himself Lord-Paramount. The pundit at Taxila had told of the fight young Vasumitra, great Pushyamitra's grandson, had with a wandering band of Yavanas when he was guarding the horse. The aged one, when a stripling, must have seen that battle. What luck!

Early next morning they crossed the flooded river by means of a raft floated on inflated bullock-skins. And now they hastened. It was a kind, generous land through which they rode. In the silver mist of dawn, quails, red and grey, ran across their paths and hares broke constantly from the cactus hedges. In the thin light of the 'wolfs brush' jackals were seen slinking home and the rising sun shone on the backs of antelopes.

Haste as they might, yet progress was slow and it was more than three months since they left Taxila when they entered Ujjjain. In green and gold, in rose-colour and snow-white, in dimples and greys, the city and its walls made a picture charming to the eye. As sang a poet of later days:

> 'Oh, fine Ujjain, Gem to Avanti given; Where village ancients tell their tales of mirth.
> And old romance; oh, radiant bit of heaven!'

Four days were spent in resting and enjoying the hospitality of the students in the college for the study of the stars. Heliodoros was enamoured with the wonderful stone instruments for measuring the heights of the heavenly bodies. Soon, too soon, he thought they moved on across the beautiful Dasharna country towards Vidisa (Bhilsa).

The sweet, sweet smell of forest earth filled their nostrils. The low bushes were aglow with buds and the trees were filled with green parrots. It was a journey of only 120 odd miles and on the seventh day they were in sight of the city. That night they camped on the banks of a lovely reed-fringed jheel, full of crimson and blue lotuses and crowded with water-birds. The next morning, they entered the city and the ambassador sought audience of the king. He was led at once to Bhagabhadra, a prince of pleasant demeanour, courteous and frank yet with a truly royal dignity.

'Victory oh King' and the Greek bowed low. 'I bring greeting from mighty Antialcidas' and he proffered the letter. It ran thus,

'The king of Taxila salutes the king of Vidisa.

The reputation of the Maharaja has spread far and wide and the benefits of his rule has reached to distant regions. So great is his fame and so powerful his strength that I, Antialcidas, Keeper of the Northern Gates, desire to make treaty with him so that north and south may be bound together in friendship and peace with prosperity abound.

Salutation.
Antialcidas.'

The letter was read and given to the chief minister; then 'What of my son?' asked the royal father. From his leather pouch Heliodoros drew the epistle entrusted to him by Bhadrasena in Taxila. The king's hand trembled as he untied the golden thread. The letter ended, 'Of Dion and his family I have only loving words to speak. They have made the wilderness to blossom for me, have treated me as a son and I ask my gracious father to give to my friend, Heliodoros, the welcome his father gave to me.'

The king stepped down, embraced the young man and said, 'As thy father dealt with my son so will I with thee.'

Thus the Greek became a member of the king's household, mixing freely with its inmates. There were two children, Malavika, a slender maid of fourteen years and Kusha, a charming, eager child, who showed 'his little buds of teeth in countless peals of laughter'.

Vidisa at this time was as beautiful as any great city of the world. The king's palace was built close to a lake and surrounded by lovely green parterres threaded with silver streams. Even in dreams Heliodoros had never seen such a wonderful structure as rose, storey above storey, in rose-red and snowy-white balconies, gay with frescoes and floral ornaments. Beneath these lay the palace-garden with its pomegranates, feathery palms and broad-flagged bananas.

It was the time of the cold weather and each day was delightful. One of the tasks imposed by Antialcidas was the gathering of many fine elephants. So, long treks were made through sombre forests and over enchanting plains. To rise at dawn, to taste the pure air flying across the maidan, to hear the cry of the sand-grouse before the bird was seen, to startle a storm of purple, green and gold as the peacocks rose from the kura grass, made a life strongly alluring to the Greek, lover of beauty in all its forms.

A year passed before the tale of elephants was complete. And now the ambassador had to select some rare and precious stones for Antialcidas. Bazaar rumours of Vidisa's jewels, of diamonds as big as a hen's egg, of pearls the size of grapes, of rubies in clusters like sultanas had spread to the north and tickled the king's ear. He would adorn his flat cap with an aigrette. So, from the south and from the diamond mines, merchants came with their stores of flashing gems for Heliodoros to inspect. After some weeks' examination he authorized three to proceed to Taxila.

The second spring of his stay was near. One early morning he walked in a small garden. At its heart was a pool where forever broke a ripple. Around the pool some trees stood. The mango cast the faint sweet scent of its modest flower on the air; the simal opened its red, red bowls for the birds to sip, and the asoka, the sorrowless tree burgeoned into spear-shaped wavy leaves. But its bright blossoms of crimson, orange and saffron were still closed and to the young man's amusement a maiden, standing in front of its sweetly dancing lines, was timidly kicking the trunk with her sandalled pink-tinted foot.

'Bravo, Malavika,' he called as he approached. 'The tree will surely blossom now the foot of such a beautiful woman has touched it.'

As swiftly she turned, her lemon-yellow sari slipped from the bee-black hair where nestled a small red rose. Under a graceful arch of brows great eyes misted over and a silver tear hung on dark lashes. Heliodoros was aghast. Never would he wound so tender a heart.

'Come,' he said. 'Remember how you married the vine to the mango tree. See how prosperous that union has been; what a pretty pair they make! The asoka will open its Heart's Ease flowers soon. Shall we come every morning to see when that happens?'

She smiled as she faltered, 'Every morning' and he saw that she was a lovely woman. The girl-child had suddenly bloomed into womanhood.

And so, unknown to the king and queen they met. She saw that he was brave to look upon her. To him she was the fairest woman God had made. In the East love grows quickly and soon each loved the other. As light faded, each evening Bhagabhadra's tenderly nurtured daughter braved the terrors of the dark and crept to the bamboo grove, there to secrete a fairy love-letter, cut by her dainty nail on a birch leaf for Heliodoros. Alas! a wanton breeze blew a letter from its hiding place and Kusha, playing near, found and took it to his mother, Savitri.

Malavika was wife-old. Already suitors had spoken for her hand. The court astrologers at this very time were busy casting the horoscopes of various princes to see with whom the princess might be auspiciously united.

With an anxious hurry the queen came to her husband and the mandate went forth—the lovers must be parted; the man banished from the palace and the maiden confined to the woman's quarters.

'She will forget if thou, wise wife, speak to her. Entreat her not to shame her father's house by caring for a barbarian. Bid her prepare to marry one of our choice.' So spoke the monarch, skilled in man's affairs but knowing not the ways of a maid.

Malavika protested not, but a palpable wistfulness settled over her, and the tear-swollen eye, the unanointed curl, the loose attire spoke in poignant language to the mother's heart. Savitri again sought her husband and with love and gentle sweetness pleaded for her daughter's happiness. 'Let us consult pundit Kaushika. He is wise. He may perchance, solicit the gods and they will show a way out of this difficulty,' she said.

'Perchance.' Bhagabhadra could not forget that it was one he had welcomed who had hurt his heart and pride. But he sent for the wise man.

'Our daughter is sick. Only a shadow of her beauty remains. Give us of thy wisdom, oh father.'

'Victory oh King! What says the queen? I know not the maiden's heart.'

'Thou art indeed wise, punditji. Her mother says she loves the Greek stranger.'

'I will talk with the young man.'

Heliodoros was eager to explain to this trusted friend of the court how love came unsought; how his birth was noble, could he not trace his descent back to a prince who had come with Alexander, how his father had great wealth; but the question came swift, 'What of thy god?'

In truth he could not name one god. All were alike, he thought but he was willing to learn and Kaushika advised his majesty to allow the marriage if the Greek would accept Vishnu as his God. On such terms the lover was more than willing to take Malavika for virtue, love and wealth.

Joyfully the mother whispered the sweet message of her father's consent to her child. 'It is good,' said the sick girl. 'A maiden cannot choose again once her troth is given. Her lips must confess what her heart holds dear.'

Brightly dawned the bridal day. A crowd of gaily clad, quickly moving people thronged the city. Festive trumpets sounded and rich festoons and graceful garlands hung from balcony and wall.

Quickly the months passed in marital bliss and the joy of man and wife was perfected by the birth of a son. Happy tears dimmed Malavika's eyes as she caressed the boy with her 'blossom-hand'. Her beauty grew till she seemed a flower unfolding in mysterious bliss.

Her husband was anxious to return to Taxila. His stay had lasted for a much longer time than was at first intended. He wished to make account of his ambassadorship of King Antialcidas. One hundred elephants were ready to go northwards. He, his wife and child would precede them and travel in comfort if they left just after the rains.

One morning his wife woke him. The babe was crying and would not be stilled. Tiny hands were clenched, little eyes glazed. The mother was frantic. Desperately she sought to ease her darling's pain. Over the fevered body the nurse cracked her thumbs. Savitri came in haste bringing the charm which cured Kasha years ago. All was of no avail.

Malavika turned to her husband. 'He is dying,' she cried. 'The gods are angry because thou dost only give lip-worship. Haste to the temple and ask what thou must do. Go, go,' and she pushed him from the chamber.

'Every prayer, which is uttered, finds its way to the ears of the Great Presence,' muttered the unhappy father as he strode swiftly to the temple. A dark-faced twice-born with dreamy emaciated face and ardent sunk eyes cast off his shoes, bared his right shoulder and covered his hands while he began in the three mystical manners to recite the sacred text. The magical words fell on the ears of Heliodoros; only to hear these chanted formulas was salvation. He felt his son would live.

Quickly he retraced his steps. 'He sleeps,' whispered Malavika. 'Krishna has blessed us.'

The father's heart filled with gratitude and he said, 'I will erect a pillar so that all men shall know how great is Krishna, incarnation of Vishnu, who has given us back our joy.'

But his wife replied, 'Heart of my heart, it is good to honour the gods but put not the child's name lest evil again befall him.'

'Nay!' said the Brahman Kaushika, who entered as they

spoke together. 'Nay, put words that will help all who pass this way. Put on the pillar these words: "Three immortal precepts lead to heaven—self-restraint, charity, conscientiousness."' And so even to this day are these precepts preserved on the column standing amid the scanty vestiges of the once-famed Vidisa.

THE GIRL ON THE TRAIN

Ruskin Bond

I had the train compartment to myself up to Rohana, then a girl got in. The couple who saw her off were probably her parents; they seemed very anxious about her comfort, and the woman gave the girl detailed instructions as to where to keep her things, when not to lean out of windows, and how to avoid speaking to strangers.

They called their goodbyes and the train pulled out of the station. As I was going blind at the time, my eyes sensitive only to light and darkness, I was unable to tell what the girl looked like; but I knew she wore slippers from the way they slapped against her heels.

It would take me some time to discover something about her looks, and perhaps I never would. But I liked the sound of her voice, and even the sound of her slippers.

'Are you going all the way to Dehra?' I asked.

I must have been sitting in a dark corner, because my voice startled her. She gave a little exclamation and said, 'I didn't know anyone else was here.'

Well, it often happens that people with good eyesight fail to see what is right in front of them. They have too much to take in, I suppose. Whereas people who cannot see (or see very little) have to take in only the essentials, whatever registers most tellingly on their remaining senses.

'I didn't see you either,' I said. 'But I heard you come in.'

I wondered if I would be able to prevent her from discovering that I was blind. Provided I keep to my seat, I thought, it shouldn't be too difficult.

The girl said, 'I'm getting off at Saharanpur. My aunt is meeting me there.'

'Then I had better not get too familiar,' I replied. 'Aunts are usually formidable creatures.'

'Where are you going?' she asked.

'To Dehra, and then to Mussoorie.'

'Oh, how lucky you are. I wish I were going to Mussoorie. I love the hills. Especially in October.'

'Yes, this is the best time,' I said, calling on my memories. 'The hills are covered with wild dahlias, the sun is delicious, and at night you can sit in front of a logfire and drink a little brandy. Most of the tourists have gone, and the roads are quiet and almost deserted. Yes, October is the best time.'

She was silent. I wondered if my words had touched her, or whether she thought me a romantic fool. Then I made a mistake.

'What is it like outside?' I asked.

She seemed to find nothing strange in the question. Had she noticed already that I could not see? But her next question removed my doubts.

'Why don't you look out of the window?' she asked.

I moved easily along the berth and felt for the window ledge. The window was open, and I faced it, making a pretence of studying the landscape. I heard the panting of the engine, the rumble of the wheels, and, in my mind's eye, I could see telegraph posts flashing by.

'Have you noticed,' I ventured, 'that the trees seem to be moving while we seem to be standing still?'

'That always happens,' she said. 'Do you see any animals?'

'No,' I answered quite confidently. I knew that there were hardly any animals left in the forests near Dehra.

I turned from the window and faced the girl, and for a while we sat in silence.

'You have an interesting face,' I remarked. I was becoming quite daring, but it was a safe remark. Few girls can resist flattery. She laughed pleasantly—a clear ringing laugh.

'It's nice to be told I have an interesting face. I'm tired of people telling me I have a pretty face.'

Oh, so you do have a pretty face, thought I; and aloud I said, 'Well, an interesting face can also be pretty.'

'You are a very gallant young man,' she said 'but why are you so serious?'

I thought, then, I would try to laugh for her, but the thought of laughter only made me feel troubled and lonely.

'We'll soon be at your station,' I said.

'Thank goodness it's a short journey. I can't bear to sit in a train for more than two or three hours.'

Yet I was prepared to sit there for almost any length of time, just to listen to her talking. Her voice had the sparkle of a mountain stream. As soon as she left the train, she would forget our brief encounter; but it would stay with me for the rest of the journey, and for some time after.

The engine's whistle shrieked, the carriage wheels changed their sound and rhythm, the girl got up and began to collect her things. I wondered if she wore her hair in a bun, or if it was plaited; perhaps it was hanging loose over her shoulders, or was it cut very short?

The train drew slowly into the station. Outside, there was the shouting of porters and vendors and a high-pitched female voice near the carriage door; that voice must have belonged to the girl's aunt.

'Goodbye,' the girl said.

She was standing very close to me, so close that the perfume from her hair was tantalizing. I wanted to raise my hand and touch her hair, but she moved away. Only the scent of perfume still lingered where she had stood.

There was some confusion in the doorway. A man, getting into the compartment, stammered an apology. Then the door banged, and the world was shut out again. I returned to my berth. The guard blew his whistle and we moved off. Once again, I had a game to play and a new fellow-traveller.

The train gathered speed, the wheels took up their song, the carriage groaned and shook. I found the window and sat in front of it, staring into the daylight that was darkness for me.

So many things were happening outside the window: it could be a fascinating game, guessing what went on out there.

The man who had entered the compartment broke into my reverie.

'You must be disappointed,' he said. 'I'm not nearly as attractive a travelling companion as the one who just left.'

'She was an interesting girl,' I said. 'Can you tell me—did she keep her hair long or short?'

'I don't remember,' he said, sounding puzzled. 'It was her eyes I noticed, not her hair. She had beautiful eyes—but they were of no use to her. She was completely blind. Didn't you notice?'

THE LAGOON

Joseph Conrad

The white man, leaning with both arms over the roof of the little house in the stern of the boat, said to the steersman—

'We will pass the night in Arsat's clearing. It is late.'

The Malay only grunted, and went on looking fixedly at the river. The white man rested his chin on his crossed arms and gazed at the wake of the boat. At the end of the straight avenue of forests cut by the intense glitter of the river, the sun appeared unclouded and dazzling, poised low over the water that shone smoothly like a band of metal. The forests, somber and dull, stood motionless and silent on each side of the broad stream. At the foot of big, towering trees, trunkless nipa palms rose from the mud of the bank, in bunches of leaves enormous and heavy, that hung unstirring over the brown swirl of eddies. In the stillness of the air every tree, every leaf, every bough, every tendril of creeper and every petal of minute blossoms seemed to have been bewitched into an immobility perfect and final. Nothing moved on the river but the eight paddles that rose flashing regularly, dipped together with a single splash; while the steersman swept right and left with a periodic and sudden flourish of his blade describing a glinting semicircle above his head. The churned-up water frothed alongside with a confused murmur. And the white man's canoe, advancing up stream in the short-lived disturbance of its own making, seemed to enter the portals of a land from which the very memory of motion had forever departed.

The white man, turning his back upon the setting sun, looked along the empty and broad expanse of the sea-reach. For the last three miles of its course the wandering, hesitating river, as if enticed irresistibly by the freedom of an open horizon, flows straight into the sea, flows straight to the east— to the east that harbours both light and darkness. Astern of the boat the repeated call of some bird, a cry discordant and feeble, skipped along over the smooth water and lost itself, before it could reach the other shore, in the breathless silence of the world.

The steersman dug his paddle into the stream, and held hard with stiffened arms, his body thrown forward. The water gurgled aloud; and suddenly the long straight reach seemed to pivot on its centre, the forests swung in a semicircle, and the slanting beams of sunset touched the broadside of the canoe with a fiery glow, throwing the slender and distorted shadows of its crew upon the streaked glitter of the river. The white man turned to look ahead. The course of the boat had been altered at right-angles to the stream, and the carved dragon-head of its prow was pointing now at a gap in the fringing bushes of the bank. It glided through, brushing the overhanging twigs, and disappeared from the river like some slim and amphibious creature leaving the water for its lair in the forests.

The narrow creek was like a ditch: tortuous, fabulously

deep; filled with gloom under the thin strip of pure and shining blue of the heaven. Immense trees soared up, invisible behind the festooned draperies of creepers. Here and there, near the glistening blackness of the water, a twisted root of some tall tree showed amongst the tracery of small ferns, black and dull, writhing and motionless, like an arrested snake. The short words of the paddlers reverberated loudly between the thick and somber walls of vegetation. Darkness oozed out from between the trees, through the tangled maze of the creepers, from behind the great fantastic and unstirring leaves; the darkness, mysterious and invincible; the darkness scented and poisonous of impenetrable forests.

The men poled in the shoaling water. The creek broadened, opening out into a wide sweep of a stagnant lagoon. The forests receded from the marshy bank, leaving a level strip of bright-green, reedy grass to frame the reflected blueness of the sky. A fleecy pink cloud drifted high above, trailing the delicate colouring of its image under the floating leaves and the silvery blossoms of the lotus. A little house, perched on high piles, appeared black in the distance. Near it, two tall nibong palms, that seemed to have come out of the forests in the background, leaned slightly over the ragged roof, with a suggestion of sad tenderness and care in the droop of their leafy and soaring heads.

The steersman, pointing with his paddle, said, 'Arsat is there. I see his canoe fast between the piles.'

The polers ran along the sides of the boat glancing over their shoulders at the end of the day's journey. They would have preferred to spend the night somewhere else than on this lagoon of weird aspect and ghostly reputation. Moreover, they disliked Arsat, first as a stranger, and also because he who repairs a ruined house, and dwells in it, proclaims that he is not afraid to live amongst the spirits that haunt the places abandoned by mankind. Such a man can disturb the course of fate by glances or words; while his familiar ghosts are not easy to propitiate by casual wayfarers upon whom they long to wreak the malice of their human master. White men care not for such things, being unbelievers and in league with the Father of Evil, who leads them unharmed through the invisible dangers of this world. To the warnings of the righteous they oppose an offensive pretence of disbelief. What is there to be done?

So they thought, throwing their weight on the end of their long poles. The big canoe glided on swiftly, noiselessly and smoothly, towards Arsat's clearing, till, in a great rattling of poles thrown down, and the loud murmurs of 'Allah be praised!' it came with a gentle knock against the crooked piles below the house.

The boatmen with uplifted faces shouted discordantly, 'Arsat! O Arsat!' Nobody came. The white man began to climb the rude ladder giving access to the bamboo platform before the house. The juragan of the boat said sulkily, 'We will cook in the sampan, and sleep on the water.'

'Pass my blankets and the basket,' said the white man curtly.

He knelt on the edge of the platform to receive the bundle. Then the boat shoved off, and the white man, standing up, confronted Arsat, who had come out through the low door of his hut. He was a man young, powerful, with a broad chest and muscular arms. He had nothing on but his sarong. His head was bare. His big, soft eyes stared eagerly at the white man, but his voice and demeanour were composed as he asked, without any words of greeting—

'Have you medicine, Tuan?'

'No,' said the visitor in a startled tone. 'No. Why? Is there sickness in the house?'

'Enter and see,' replied Arsat, in the same calm manner, and turning short round, passed again through the small doorway. The white man, dropping his bundles, followed.

In the dim light of the dwelling he made out on a couch of bamboos a woman stretched on her back under a broad sheet of red cotton cloth. She lay still, as if dead; but her big eyes, wide open, glittered in the gloom, staring upwards at the slender rafters, motionless and unseeing. She was in a high fever, and evidently unconscious. Her cheeks were sunk slightly, her lips were partly open, and on the young face there was the ominous and fixed expression—the absorbed, contemplating expression of the unconscious who are going to die. The two men stood looking down at her in silence.

'Has she been long ill?' asked the traveller.

'I have not slept for five nights,' answered the Malay, in a deliberate tone. 'At first she heard voices calling her from the water and struggled against me who held her. But since the sun of today rose she hears nothing—she hears not me. She sees nothing. She sees not me—me!'

He remained silent for a minute, then asked softly—

'Tuan, will she die?'

'I fear so,' said the white man sorrowfully. He had known Arsat years ago, in a far country in times of trouble and danger, when no friendship is to be despised. And since his Malay friend had come unexpectedly to dwell in the hut on the lagoon with a strange woman, he had slept many times there, in his journeys up or down the river. He liked the man who knew how to keep faith in council and how to fight without fear by the side of his white friend. He liked him—not so much perhaps as a man likes his favourite dog—but still he liked him well enough to help and ask no questions, to think sometimes vaguely and hazily in the midst of his own pursuits, about the lonely man and the long-haired woman with audacious face and triumphant eyes, who lived together hidden by the forests—alone and feared.

The white man came out of the hut in time to see the enormous conflagration of sunset put out by the swift and stealthy shadows that, rising like a black and impalpable vapour above the tree-tops, spread over the heaven, extinguishing the crimson glow of floating clouds and the red brilliance of departing daylight. In a few moments all the stars came out above the intense blackness of the earth, and the great lagoon gleaming suddenly with reflected lights resembled an oval patch of night-sky flung down into the hopeless and abysmal night of the wilderness. The white man had some supper out of the basket, then collecting a few sticks that lay about the platform, made up a small fire, not for warmth, but for the sake of the smoke, which would keep off the mosquitoes. He wrapped himself in his blankets and sat with his back against the reed wall of the house, smoking thoughtfully.

Arsat came through the doorway with noiseless steps and squatted down by the fire. The white man moved his outstretched legs a little.

'She breathes,' said Arsat in a low voice, anticipating the expected question. 'She breathes and burns as if with a great fire. She speaks not; she hears not—and burns!'

He paused for a moment, then asked in a quiet, incurious tone—

'Tuan...will she die?'

The white man moved his shoulders uneasily, and muttered in a hesitating manner—

'If such is her fate.'

'No, Tuan,' said Arsat calmly. 'If such is my fate. I hear, I see, I wait. I remember... Tuan, do you remember the old days? Do you remember my brother?'

'Yes,' said the white man. The Malay rose suddenly and went in. The other, sitting still outside, could hear the voice in the hut. Arsat said: 'Hear me! Speak!' His words were succeeded by a complete silence. 'O! Diamelen!' he cried suddenly. After that cry there was a deep sigh. Arsat came out and sank down again in his old place.

They sat in silence before the fire. There was no sound within the house, there was no sound near them; but far away on the lagoon they could hear the voices of the boatmen ringing fitful and distinct on the calm water. The fire in the bows of the sampan shone faintly in the distance with a hazy red glow. Then it died out. The voices ceased. The land and the water slept invisible, unstirring and mute. It was as though there had been nothing left in the world but the glitter of stars streaming, ceaseless and vain, through the black stillness of the night.

The white man gazed straight before him into the darkness with wide-open eyes. The fear and fascination, the inspiration and the wonder of death—of death near, unavoidable and unseen, soothed the unrest of his race and stirred the most indistinct, the most intimate of his thoughts. The ever-ready suspicion of evil, the gnawing suspicion that lurks in our hearts, flowed out into the stillness round him—into the stillness profound and dumb, and made it appear untrustworthy and infamous, like the placid and impenetrable mask of an unjustifiable violence. In that fleeting and powerful disturbance of his being the earth enfolded in the starlight peace became a shadowy country of inhuman strife, a battlefield of phantoms terrible and charming, august or ignoble, struggling ardently for the possession of our helpless hearts. An unquiet and mysterious country of inextinguishable desires and fears.

A plaintive murmur rose in the night; a murmur saddening and startling, as if the great solitudes of surrounding woods had tried to whisper into his ear the wisdom of their immense and lofty indifference. Sounds hesitating and vague floated in the air round him, shaped themselves slowly into words; and at last flowed on gently in a murmuring stream of soft and monotonous sentences. He stirred like a man waking up and changed his position slightly. Arsat, motionless and shadowy, sitting with bowed head under the stars, was speaking in a low and dreamy tone.

'... for where can we lay down the heaviness of our trouble but in a friend's heart? A man must speak of war and of love. You, Tuan, know what war is, and you have seen me in time of danger seek death as other men seek life! A writing may be lost; a lie may be written; but what the eye has seen is truth and remains in the mind!'

'I remember,' said the white man quietly. Arsat went on with mournful composure.

'Therefore I shall speak to you of love. Speak in the night. Speak before both night and love are gone—and the eye of day looks upon my sorrow and my shame; upon my blackened face; upon my burnt-up heart.'

A sigh, short and faint, marked an almost imperceptible

pause, and then his words flowed on, without a stir, without a gesture.

'After the time of trouble and war was over and you went away from my country in the pursuit of your desires, which we, men of the islands, cannot understand, I and my brother became again, as we had been before, the sword-bearers of the Ruler. You know we were men of family, belonging to a ruling race, and more fit than any to carry on our right shoulder the emblem of power. And in the time of prosperity Si Dendring showed us favour, as we, in time of sorrow, had showed to him the faithfulness of our courage. It was a time of peace. A time of deer-hunts and cock-fights; of idle talks and foolish squabbles between men whose bellies are full and weapons are rusty. But the sower watched the young rice-shoots grow up without fear, and the traders came and went, departed lean and returned fat into the river of peace. They brought news too. Brought lies and truth mixed together, so that no man knew when to rejoice and when to be sorry. We heard from them about you also. They had seen you here and had seen you there. And I was glad to hear, for I remembered the stirring times, and I always remembered you, Tuan, till the time came when my eyes could see nothing in the past, because they had looked upon the one who is dying there—in the house.'

He stopped to exclaim in an intense whisper, 'O Mara bahia! O Calamity!' then went on speaking a little louder.

'There's no worse enemy and no better friend than a brother, Tuan, for one brother knows another, and in perfect knowledge is strength for good or evil. I loved my brother. I went to him and told him that I could see nothing but one face, hear nothing but one voice. He told me: "Open your heart so that she can see what is in it—and wait. Patience is wisdom. Inchi Midah may die or our Ruler may throw off his fear of a woman!"...I waited! You remember the lady with the veiled face, Tuan, and the fear of our Ruler before her cunning and temper. And if she wanted her servant, what could I do? But I fed the hunger of my heart on short glances and stealthy words. I loitered on the path to the bath-houses in the daytime, and when the sun had fallen behind the forest I crept along the jasmine hedges of the women's courtyard. Unseeing, we spoke to one another through the scent of flowers, through the veil of leaves, through the blades of long grass that stood still before our lips: so great was our prudence, so faint was the murmur of our great longing. The time passed swiftly ... and there were whispers amongst women—and our enemies watched—my brother was gloomy, and I began to think of killing and of a fierce death... We are of a people who take what they want—like you whites. There is a time when a man should forget loyalty and respect. Might and authority are given to rulers, but to all men is given love and strength and courage. My brother said, "You shall take her from their midst. We are two who are like one." And I answered, "Let it be soon, for I find no warmth in sunlight that does not shine upon her." Our time came when the Ruler and all the great people went to the mouth of the river to fish by torchlight. There were hundreds of boats, and on the white sand, between the water and the forests, dwellings of leaves were built for the households of the Rajahs. The smoke of cooking-fires was like a blue mist of the evening, and many voices rang in it joyfully. While they were making the boats ready to beat up the fish, my brother came to me and said, "Tonight!" I made ready my weapons, and when the time came our canoe took its place in the circle of boats carrying the torches. The lights blazed on the water, but behind the boats there was darkness. When the shouting began and the excitement made them like mad we dropped out. The water swallowed our fire, and we floated back to the shore that was dark with only here and there the glimmer of embers. We could hear the talk of slavegirls amongst the sheds. Then we found a place deserted and silent. We waited there. She came. She came running along the shore, rapid and leaving no trace, like a leaf driven by the wind into the sea. My brother said gloomily, "Go and take her; carry her into our boat." I lifted her in my arms. She panted. Her heart was beating against my breast. I said, "I take you from those people. You came to the cry of my heart, but my arms take you into my boat against the will of the great!"

"It is right," said my brother. "We are men who take what we want and can hold it against many. We should have taken her in daylight."

'I said, "Let us be off;" for since she was in my boat I began to think of our Ruler's many men.

"Yes. Let us be off," said my brother. "We are cast out and this boat is our country now—and the sea is our refuge." He lingered with his foot on the shore, and I entreated him to hasten, for I remembered the strokes of her heart against my breast and thought that two men cannot withstand a hundred. We left, paddling downstream close to the bank; and as we passed by the creek where they were fishing, the great shouting had ceased, but the murmur of voices was loud like the humming of insects flying at noonday. The boats floated, clustered together, in the red light of torches, under a black roof of smoke; and men talked of their sport. Men that boasted, and praised, and jeered—men that would have been our friends in the morning, but on that night were already our enemies. We paddled swiftly past. We had no more friends in the country of our birth. She sat in the middle of the canoe with covered face; silent as she is now; unseeing as she is now—and I had no regret at what I was leaving because I could hear her breathing close to me—as I can hear her now.'

He paused, listened with his ear turned to the doorway, then shook his head and went on.

'My brother wanted to shout the cry of challenge—one cry only—to let the people know we were freeborn robbers that trusted our arms and the great sea. And again I begged him in the name of our love to be silent. Could I not hear her breathing close to me? I knew the pursuit would come quick enough. My brother loved me. He dipped his paddle without a splash. He only said, "There is half a man in you now—the other half is in that woman. I can wait. When you are a whole man again, you will come back with me here to shout defiance. We are sons of the same mother." I made no answer.

'All my strength and all my spirit were in my hands that held the paddle—for I longed to be with her in a safe place beyond the reach of men's anger and of women's spite. My love was so great, that I thought it could guide me to a country where death was unknown, if I could only escape from Inchi Midah's spite and from our Ruler's sword. We paddled with fury, breathing through our teeth. The blades bit deep into the smooth water. We passed out of the river; we flew in clear channels amongst the shallows. We skirted the black coast; we skirted the sand beaches where the sea speaks in whispers to the land; and the gleam of white sand flashed back past our boat, so swiftly she ran upon the water.

We spoke not. Only once I said, "Sleep, Diamelen, for soon you may want all your strength." I heard the sweetness of her voice, but I never turned my head. The sun rose and still we went on. Water fell from my face like rain from a cloud. We flew in the light and heat. I never looked back, but I knew that my brother's eyes, behind me, were looking steadily ahead, for the boat went as straight as a bushman's dart, when it leaves the end of the sumpitan. There was no better paddler, no better steersman than my brother. Many times, together, we had won races in that canoe. But we never had put out our strength as we did then—then, when for the last time we paddled together! There was no braver or stronger man in our country than my brother. I could not spare the strength to turn my head and look at him, but every moment I heard the hiss of his breath getting louder behind me. Still he did not speak. The sun was high. The heat clung to my back like a flame of fire. My ribs were ready to burst, but I could no longer get enough air into my chest. And then I felt I must cry out with my last breath, "Let us rest!"

"'Good!' he answered; and his voice was firm. He was strong. He was brave. He knew not fear and no fatigue... My brother!'

A rumour powerful and gentle, a rumour vast and faint; the rumour of trembling leaves, of stirring boughs, ran through the tangled depths of the forests, ran over the starry smoothness of the lagoon, and the water between the piles lapped the slimy timber once with a sudden splash. A breath of warm air touched the two men's faces and passed on with a mournful sound—a breath loud and short like an uneasy sigh of the dreaming earth.

Arsat went on in an even, low voice.

'We ran our canoe on the white beach of a little bay close to a long tongue of land that seemed to bar our road; a long wooded cape going far into the sea. My brother knew that place. Beyond the cape a river has its entrance. Through the jungle of that land there is a narrow path. We made a fire and cooked rice. Then we slept on the soft sand in the shade of our canoe, while she watched. No sooner had I closed my eyes than I heard her cry of alarm. We leaped up. The sun was halfway down the sky already, and coming in sight in the opening of the bay we saw a prau manned by many paddlers. We knew it at once; it was one of our Rajah's praus. They were watching the shore, and saw us. They beat the gong, and turned the head of the prau into the bay. I felt my heart become weak within my breast. Diamelen sat on the sand and covered her face. There was no escape by sea.

'My brother laughed. He had the gun you had given him, Tuan, before you went away, but there was only a handful of powder. He spoke to me quickly: "Run with her along the path. I shall keep them back, for they have no firearms, and landing in the face of a man with a gun is certain death for some. Run with her. On the other side of that wood there is a fisherman's house—and a canoe. When I have fired all the shots I will follow. I am a great runner, and before they can come up we shall be gone. I will hold out as long as I can, for she is but a woman—that can neither run nor fight, but she has your heart in her weak hands." He dropped behind the canoe. The prau was coming. She and I ran, and as we rushed along the path I heard shots. My brother fired—once—twice—and the booming of the gong ceased. There was silence behind us. That neck of land is narrow. Before I heard my brother fire the third shot I saw the shelving shore, and I saw the water again: the mouth of a broad river. We crossed a grassy glade. We ran down to the water. I saw a low hut above the black mud, and a small canoe hauled up. I heard another shot behind me. I thought, "That is his last charge." We rushed down to the canoe; a man came running from the hut, but I leaped on him, and we rolled together in the mud. Then I got up, and he lay still at my feet. I don't know whether I had killed him or not. I and Diamelen pushed the canoe afloat. I heard yells behind me, and I saw my brother run across the glade. Many men were bounding after him. I took her in my arms and threw her into the boat, then leaped in myself. When I looked back I saw that my brother had fallen. He fell and was up again, but the men were closing round him. He shouted, "I am coming!" The men were close to him. I looked. Many men. Then I looked at her. Tuan, I pushed the canoe! I pushed it into deep water. She was kneeling forward looking at me, and I said, "Take your paddle," while I struck the water with mine. Tuan, I heard him cry. I heard him cry my name twice; and I heard voices shouting, "Kill! Strike!" I never turned back. I heard him calling my name again with a great shriek, as when life is going out together with the voice—and I never turned my head. My own name! My brother! Three times he called—but I was not afraid of life. Was she not there in that canoe? And could I not with her find a country where death is forgotten—where death is unknown?'

The white man sat up. Arsat rose and stood, an indistinct and silent figure above the dying embers of the fire. Over the lagoon a mist drifting and low had crept, erasing slowly the glittering images of the stars. And now a great expanse of white vapour covered the land: flowed cold and grey in the darkness, eddied in noiseless whirls round the tree-trunks and about the platform of the house, which seemed to float upon a restless and impalpable illusion of a sea; seemed the only thing surviving the destruction of the world by that undulating and voiceless phantom of a flood. Only far away the tops of the trees stood outlined on the twinkle of heaven, like a somber and forbidding shore—a coast deceptive, pitiless and black.

Arsat's voice vibrated loudly in the profound peace.

'I had her there! I had her! To get her I would have faced all mankind. But I had her—and—'

His words went out ringing into the empty distances. He paused, and seemed to listen to them dying away very far—beyond help and beyond recall. Then he said quietly—

'Tuan, I loved my brother.'

A breath of wind made him shiver. High above his head, high above the silent sea of mist the drooping leaves of the palms rattled together with a mournful and expiring sound. The white man stretched his legs. His chin rested on his chest, and he murmured sadly without lifting his head—

'We all love our brothers.'

Arsat burst out with an intense whispering violence—

'What did I care who died? I wanted peace in my own heart.'

He seemed to hear a stir in the house—listened—then stepped in noiselessly. The white man stood up. A breeze was coming in fitful puffs. The stars shone paler as if they had retreated into the frozen depths of immense space. After a chill gust of wind there were a few seconds of perfect calm and absolute silence. Then from behind the black and wavy line of the forests a column of golden light shot up into the heavens and spread over the semicircle of the eastern horizon. The sun had risen. The mist lifted, broke into drifting patches, vanished into thin flying wreaths; and the unveiled lagoon lay, polished and black, in the heavy shadows at the foot of the wall of trees. A white eagle rose over it with a slanting and ponderous flight, reached the clear sunshine and appeared dazzlingly brilliant for a moment, then soaring higher, became a dark and motionless speck before it vanished into the blue as if it had left the earth for ever. The white man, standing gazing upwards before the doorway, heard in the hut a confused and broken murmur of distracted words ending with a loud groan. Suddenly Arsat stumbled out with outstretched hands, shivered, and stood still for some time with fixed eyes. Then he said—

'She burns no more.'

Before his face the sun showed its edge above the treetops, rising steadily. The breeze freshened; a great brilliance burst upon the lagoon, sparkled on the rippling water. The forests came out of the clear shadows of the morning, became distinct, as if they had rushed nearer—to stop short in a great stir of leaves, of nodding boughs, of swaying branches. In the merciless sunshine the whisper of unconscious life grew louder, speaking in an incomprehensible voice round the dumb darkness of that human sorrow. Arsat's eyes wandered slowly, then stared at the rising sun.

'I can see nothing,' he said half aloud to himself.

'There is nothing,' said the white man, moving to the edge of the platform and waving his hand to his boat. A shout came faintly over the lagoon and the sampan began to glide towards the abode of the friend of ghosts.

'If you want to come with me, I will wait all the morning,' said the white man, looking away upon the water.

'No, Tuan,' said Arsat softly. 'I shall not eat or sleep in this house, but I must first see my road. Now I can see nothing—see nothing! There is no light and no peace in the world; but there is death—death for many. We were sons of the same mother—and I left him in the midst of enemies; but I am going back now.'

He drew a long breath and went on in a dreamy tone.

'In a little while I shall see clear enough to strike—to strike. But she has died, and...now...darkness.'

He flung his arms wide open, let them fall along his body, then stood still with unmoved face and stony eyes, staring at the sun. The white man got down into his canoe. The polers ran smartly along the sides of the boat, looking over their shoulders at the beginning of a weary journey. High in the stern, his head muffled up in white rags, the juragan sat moody, letting his paddle trail in the water. The white man, leaning with both arms over the grass roof of the little cabin, looked back at the shining ripple of the boat's wake. Before the sampan passed out of the lagoon into the creek he lifted his eyes. Arsat had not moved. In the searching clearness of crude sunshine he was still standing before the house, he was still looking through the great light of a cloudless day into the hopeless darkness of the world.

THE BOX TUNNEL

Charles Reade

The 10.15 train glided from Paddington, 7 May 1847. In the left compartment of a certain first-class carriage were four passengers; of these two were worth description. The lady had a smooth, white, delicate brow, strongly marked eyebrows, long lashes, eyes that seemed to change colour, and a good-sized delicious mouth, with teeth as white as milk. A man could not see her nose for her eyes and mouth; her own sex could and would have told us some nonsense about it. She wore an upretending greyish dress buttoned to the throat with lozenge-shaped buttons, and a Scottish shawl that agreeably evaded colour. She was like a duck, so tight her plain feathers fitted her, and there she sat, smooth, snug, and delicious, with a book in her hand, and the soupcon of her wrist just visible as she held it. Her opposite neighbour was what I call a good style of man—the more to his credit, since he belonged to a corporation that frequently turns out the worst imaginable style of young men. He was a cavalry officer, aged twenty-five. He had a moustache, but not a very, repulsive one; not one of those subnasal pigtails on which soup is suspended like dew on a shrub; it was short, thick, and black as a coal. His teeth had not yet been turned by tobacco smoke to the colour of juice, his clothes did not stick to nor hang to him, he had an engaging smile, and, what I liked the dog for, his vanity, which was inordinate, was in its proper place, his heart, not in his face, jostling mine and other people's who have none; in a word, he was what one often hears of than meets—a young gentleman.

He was conversing in an animated whisper with a companion, a fellow-officer; they were talking about what it is far better not to—women. Our friend clearly did not wish to be overheard; for he cast ever and anon a furtive glance at his fair *vis-a-vis* and lowered his voice. She seemed completely absorbed in her book, and that reassured him.

At last the two soldiers came down to a whisper (the truth must be told); the one who got down at Slough, and was lost to posterity, her ten pounds to three that he who was going down with us to Bath and immortality would not kiss either of the ladies opposite upon the road. 'Done, done!'

Now, I am sorry, a man I have hitherto praised should have lent himself, even in a whisper, to such a speculation; 'but nobody is wise at all hours,' not even when the clock is striking five-and-twenty; and you are to consider his profession, his good looks, and the temptation—ten to three.

After Slough the party was reduced to three; at Twyford one lady dropped her handkerchief; Captain Dolignan fell on it like a lamb; two or three words were interchanged on this occasion.

At Reading, the Marlborough of our tale made one of the safe investments of that day, he bought *Times* and *Punch;* the latter full of steel-pen thrusts and wood-cuts. Valour and beauty deigned to laugh at some inflamed humbug or other, punctured by *Punch*. Now laughing together thaws our human ice; long before Swindon it was a talking-match—at Swindon who so devoted as Captain Dolignan? He handed them out—he souped them, he tough-chickened them, he brandied and cochinealed one, and brandied and burnt-sugared the other; on their return to the carriage, one lady passed into the inner compartment to inspect a certain gentleman's seat on that side of the line.

Reader, had it been you or I, the beauty would have been the deserter, the average one would have stayed with us till all was blue, ourselves included; not more surely does our slice of bread and butter, when it escapes from our hand, revolve it ever so often, alight face downward on the carpet.

But this was a bit of a fop, Adonis, dragoon—so Venus remained *tole-it-fete* with him. You have seen a dog meet an unknown female of the species; how handsome, how *impresse*, how expressive he becomes; such was Dolignan after Swindon, and to do the dog justice, he got handsomer and handsomer; and you have seen a cat conscious of approaching cream—such was Miss Haythorn; she became demurer and demurer; presently our captain looked out of the window and laughed; this elicited an inquiring look from Miss Haythorn.

'We are only a mile from the Box Tunnel.'

'Do you always laugh a mile from the Box Tunnel?' said the lady.

'Invariably.'

'What for?'

'Why, hem! It is a gentleman's joke.'

Captain Dolignan then recounted to Miss Haythorn the following:

'A lady and her husband sat together going through the Box Tunnel—there was one gentleman opposite; it was pitch dark; after the tunnel the lady said, 'George, how absurd of you to salute me going through the tunnel.'

'I did no such thing.'

'You didn't?'

'No! Why?'

'Because somehow I thought you did!"

Here Captain Dolignan laughed and endeavoured to lead his companion to laugh, but it was not to be done. The train entered the tunnel.

Miss Haaythorn: Ah!

Dolignan: What is the matter?

Miss Haythorn: I am frightened.

Dolignan (moving to her side): Pray do not be alarmed; I am near you.

Miss Haythorn: You are near me—very near me, indeed, Captain Dolignan.

Dolignan: You know my name?

Miss Haythorn: I heard you mention it. I wish we were out of this dark place.

Dolignan: I could be content to spend hours here, reassuring you, my dear lady.

Miss Haythorn: Nonsense!

Dolignan: Pweep! (Grave reader, do not put your lips to the next pretty creature you meet or you will understand what this means.)

Miss Haythorn: Eh! Eh!

Friend: What is the matter?

Miss Haythorn: Open the door! Open the door!

There was a sound of hurried whispers, the door was shut

and the blind pulled down with hostile sharpness.

If any critic falls on me for putting inarticulate sounds in a dialogue as above, I answer with all the insolence I can command at present, 'Hit boys as big as yourself'; bigger perhaps, such as Sophocles, Euripides, and Aristophanes; they began it, and I learned it of them, sore against my will.

Miss Haythorn's scream lost most of its effect because the engine whistled forty thousand murders at the same moment; and fictitious grief makes itself heard when real cannot.

Between the tunnel and Bath our young friend had time to ask himself whether his conduct had been marked by that delicate reserve which is supposed to distinguish the perfect gentleman.

With a long face, real or feigned, he held open the door; his late friends attempted to escape on the other side—impossible! They must pass him. She whom he had insulted (Latin for kissed) deposited somewhere at his feet a look of gentle, blushing reproach; the other, whom he had not insulted, darted red-hot daggers at him from her eyes; and so they parted.

It was perhaps fortunate for Dolignan that he had the grace to be a friend of Major Hoskyns of his regiment, a veteran laughed at by the youngsters, for the major was too apt to look coldly upon billiard-balls and cigars; he had seen cannonballs and linstocks. He had also, to tell the truth, swallowed a good bit of the mess-room poker, which made it impossible for Major Hoskyns to descend to an ungentleman-like word or action as to brush his own trousers below the knee.

Captain Dolignan told this gentleman his story in gleeful accents; but Major Hoskyns heard him coldly, and as coldly answered that he had known a man to lose his life for the same thing.

'That is nothing,' continued the Major, 'but unfortunately he deserved to lose it.'

At this, blood mounted to the younger man's temples; and his senior added, 'I mean to say he was thirty-five; you, I presume, are twenty-one!'

'Twenty-five.'

'That is much the same thing; will you be advised by me?'

'If you will advise me.'

'Speak to no one of this, and send White the £3, that he may think you have lost the bet.'

'That is hard, when I won it.'

'Do it for all that, sir.'

Let the disbelievers in human perfectibility know that this dragoon capable of a blush, did this virtuous action, albeit with violent reluctance; and this was his first damper. A week after these events he was at a ball. He was in that state of factious discontent which belongs to us amiable English. He was looking in vain for a lady, equal in personal attraction to the idea he had formed of George Dolignan as a man, when suddenly there glided past him a most delightful vision! A lady whose beauty and symmetry took him by the eyes—another look: 'It can't be! Yes, it is!' Miss Haythorn! (not that he knew her name!) but what an apotheosis!

The duck had become a peahen—radiant, dazzling, she looked twice as beautiful and almost twice as large as before. He lost sight of her. He found her again. She was so lovely she made him ill—and he, alone, must not dance with her, speak to her. If he had been content to begin her acquaintance the usual way, it might have ended in kissing;

it must end in nothing.

As she danced, sparks of beauty fell from her all around, but him—she did not see him; it was clear she never would see him—one gentleman was particularly assiduous; she smiled on his assiduity; he was ugly, but she smiled on him. Dolignan was surprised at his success, his ill-taste, his ugliness, his impertinence. Dolignan at last found himself injured: 'Who was this man? And what right had he to go on so? He never kissed her, I suppose,' said Dolle. Dolignan could not prove it, but he felt that somehow the rights of property were invaded.

He went home and dreamed of Miss Haythorn, and hated all the ugly success. He spent a fortnight trying to find out who his beauty was—he never could encounter her again. At last, he heard of her in this way: A lawyer's clerk paid him a little visit and commenced a little action against him in the name of Miss Haythorn, for insulting her in a railway-train.

The young gentleman was shocked; endeavoured to soften the lawyer's clerk; that machine did not thoroughly comprehend the meaning of the term. The lady's name, however, was at last revealed by this untoward incident; from her name to her address was but a short step; and the same day our crestfallen hero lay in wait at her door, and many a succeeding day, without effect.

But one fine afternoon she issued forth quite naturally, as if she did it every day, and walked briskly on the parade. Dolignan did the same, met and passed her many times on the parade, and searched for pity in her eyes, but found neither look nor recognition, nor any other sentiment; for all this she walked and walked; till all the other promenaders were tired and gone—then her culprit summoned resolution, and taking off his hat, with a voice for the first time tremulous, besought permission to address her.

She stopped, blushed, and neither acknowledged nor disowned his acquaintance. He blushed, stammered out how ashamed he was, how he deserved to be punished, how he was punished, how little she knew how unhappy he was, and concluded by begging her not to let all the world know the disgrace of a man who was already mortified enough by the loss of her acquaintance.

She asked an explanation; he told her of the action that had been commenced in her name; she gently shrugged her shoulders and said, 'How stupid they are!' Emboldened by this, he begged to know whether or not a life of distant unpretending devotion would, after a lapse of years, erase the memory of his madness—his crime!

'She did not know!'

'She must now bid him adieu, as she had preparations to make for a ball in the Crescent, where everybody was to be.'

They parted, and Dolignan determined to be at the ball, where everybody was to be. He was there, and after some time he obtained an introduction to Miss Haythorn, and he danced with her. Her manner was gracious. With the wonderful tact of her sex, she seemed to have commenced the acquaintance that evening.

That night, for the first time, Dolignan was in love. I will spare the reader all a lover's arts, by which he succeeded in dining where she dined, in dancing where she danced, in overtaking her by accident when she rode. His devotion followed her to church, where the dragoon was rewarded by learning there is a world where they neither polk nor smoke—the two capital abominations of this one.

He made an acquaintance with her uncle, who liked him, and he saw at last with joy that her eye loved to dwell upon him, when she thought he did not observe her. It was three months after the Box Tunnel that Captain Dolignan called one day upon Captain Haythorn, R.N., whom he had met twice in his life, and slightly propitiated by violently listening to a cutting-out expedition; he called, and in the usual way asked permission to pay his addresses to his daughter.

The worthy captain straightaway began doing quarter-deck, when suddenly he was summoned from the apartment by a mysterious message. On his return he announced, with a total change of voice, that 'It was all right, and his visitor might run alongside as soon as he chose.' My reader has divined the truth; this nautical commander was in complete and happy subjugation to his daughter, our heroine.

As he was taking leave, Dolignan saw his divinity glide into the drawing-room. He followed her, observed a sweet consciousness deepen into confusion—she tried to laugh and cried instead, and then she smiled again; when he kissed her hand at the door it was 'George' and 'Marian' instead of 'Captain' this and 'Miss' the other.

A reasonable time after this (for my tale is merciful and skips formalities and torturing delays), these two were very happy; they were once more upon the railroad, going to enjoy their honeymoon all by themselves. Marian Dolignan was dressed just as before—duck-like and delicious; all bright except her clothes; but George sat beside her this time instead of opposite; and she drank him in gently from her long eyelashes.

'Marian,' said George, 'married people should tell each other all. Will you ever forgive me if I own to you; no—'

'Yes! Yes!'

'Well, then, you remember the Box Tunnel.' (This was the first allusion he had ventured to it.) 'I am ashamed to say I had £3 to £10 with White I would kiss one of you two lades.' And George, pathetic externally, chuckled within.

'I know that, George; I overheard you,' was the demure reply.

'Oh! You overheard me! Impossible.'

'And did you not hear me whisper to my companion? I made a bet with her.'

'You made a bet! How singular! What was it'

'Only a pair of gloves, George.'

'Yes, I know; but what about it?'

'That if you did, you should be my husband, dearest.'

'Oh! But stay; then you could not have been so very angry with me, love. Why, dearest, then you brought that action against me.'

Mrs Dolignan looked down.

'I was afraid you were forgetting me! George, you will never forgive me!'

'Angel! Why, here is the Box Tunnel!'

Now reader—fie! No! No such thing! You can't expect to be indulged in this way every time we come to a dark place. Besides, it is not the thing. Consider, two sensible married people. No scream in hopeless rivalry of the engine—this time!